FLORA ?,
JUNE 2006

Aunt Vyrnetta

and other stories from Cedar Grove...

By

Kelly Swanson

2003

Parkway Publishers, Inc.
Boone, North Carolina

Available from:

Parkway Publishers, Inc.

P. O. Box 3678

Boone, North Carolina 28607

Telephone/Facsimile: (828) 265-3993

www.parkwaypublishers.com

Library of Congress Cataloging in Publication Data

Swanson, Kelly
Aunt Vyrnetta and other stories from Cedar Grove / by Kelly Swanson.
p. cm.
ISBN 1-887905-79-0
1. Southern States--Social life and customs--Fiction. I. Title.
PS3619.W363 A96 2004
813'.6-dc22
2003018598

Editing, Layout and Book Design: Julie Shissler
Cover Design: Aaron Burleson

To my readers,

Cedar Grove is a tiny town about a mile and a hair past nowhere. They've got two stoplights total and an old brick schoolhouse that also serves as the town hall and bingo headquarters on Thursdays. They don't play for real money of course, being a town built around a Baptist Church and all. Time rolls at a slow pace in Cedar Grove, where the most exciting thing that ever happened was the time Cleetus Harley's pig made the front page of the paper for having borned her a piglet with three tails. These stories aren't fancy, they're just about the people.

You won't find the world's greatest scholars in the pages of this book. More like Booker Diggs who loves fishing, or Aunt Bitsy and her conquerin' fear idear. Please don't look in these pages for life's answers. I'm still not quite sure I've figured out all the questions. I simply love to tell a story. Stories about people. Stories about life as some of us know it.

Many of you have already met some of these wonderful people from Cedar Grove because, while it is a great joy to write about these wonderful characters that live in my head, I get an even greater joy performing these stories. Cedar Grove has been to churches and schools, garden clubs and business meetings, libraries and festivals, and even on the radio in a series of shows that aired on WPETam950.

The first four stories of this book are on my CD, *Aunt Vyrnetta and Other Stories from Cedar Grove*, which can be ordered from my website or by mail. I hope you will come to love these characters as much as I do.

With warmest thanks,

Kelly Swanson, Author and Storyteller
www.kellyswanson.net
kelly@kellyswanson.net
336-889-9479
1400 Chatham Drive
High Point, NC 27265

Table Of Contents

John Henry Junior and the
Final Battle of Cedar Grove

Did I ever tell you about John Henry Junior and the final battle of Cedar Grove? It's not something you're likely to read about in the history books but ask anybody who was there at the grand opening of the Cedar Grove Post Office and they'll tell you the story. They'll probably start with how impressive that new post office was with its wide columns and red brick. And then they'll probably tell you about the genuine bronze statue out front — Mayor Percival Peabody sitting on a horse with its front hooves reared up in the air. And then they'll most definitely point to an imprint in the cement beside that statue. An imprint of a kid's body sprawled out like an angel print in the snow. And they'll probably shake their heads and tell you that, like most trouble in that town, it all started with Jonathan Abraham Henry, Junior. And they'll be speaking the truth.

It was somewhere in between the flood that wiped out Old Man Byerly's place and the time Cleetus Harley's pig made front page of the paper for having borned her a piglet with three tails. It happened when Sam Jones's grandpa died and left him a considerable amount of money, which he decided to donate to the town to use where he best saw fit.

Thing was, Sam Jones didn't get out much; only place he ever went was to buy food and to check his mail. And seeing as how he never did care for Frank Peabody who owned the grocery, he decided a new post office would suit him just fine. And there was enough money to build what would turn out to be the biggest building in Cedar Grove until years later, when they decided it wasn't right that the church wasn't the biggest building in town. I mean, what kind of point were they trying to make? And so they added one more room on to the Cedar Grove Baptist Church until it was the biggest. But anyway, for the time being this new post office was big news. So big they hired a construction team, hard hats and all — more foreigners than Cedar Grove had ever seen in one place at one time. Bringing tools with 'em like nothing they'd ever seen before. Giant dangerous-looking metal monsters with sharp claws that ate away at the red dirt. And loud they were. So loud you could barely hear yourself order the corned beef and cabbage lunch special over at Ray Jean's Diner. For weeks that new post office was all the talk.

Folks made a point to walk past it whenever they could to keep up on the progress and put their two cents in.

"Looks kind of crooked," you'd hear someone say.

"Don't look like enough nails in that corner over there. Buster, better go over and take a look. See if'n they need some help."

"I say, Myrna, that man is sure to fall to his death walking on that beam like that. Ain't even watching where he's going. And no shirt, with the sun scorching the way it is. I'd best get him some of my homemade salve for the burn. And I declare if that youngun over there don't need him a belt something fierce! Why there's just some things ain't made for the public to see!"

Yep, folks were mighty proud of that new post office but no one got more enjoyment out of it than John Henry Jr. and the other younguns of Cedar Grove. 'Cause every night after the men had gone home and the machines were cut off, they left behind these big old mounds of red dirt — the soft kind of dirt that squishes in between your toes like baby powder.

Those younguns spent all their free time there playing a game they made up called War. Simple enough game it was. They had two sides, one against the other, and they carried around sticks and shot each other and dropped down dead in the dirt. They hid behind the dirt mounds and reloaded their stick weapons. They made cannons out of chicken wire covered in black paper and tore up old sheets to wrap their imaginary wounds. They planned strategies and attacks and even made uniforms out of some old suits they found in Luther's grandma's attic. They had all kinds of fun playing war for hours on end. But nobody took the game more seriously than John Henry Junior or Captain Henry, as he insisted on being called for weeks. To John Henry, it wasn't a game. He was a Captain. And he'd never been him a captain before; a title he would defend to the death.

But the other kids started losing interest and the game started wearing out as even the best games tend to do. The project was nearing completion and there just wasn't enough dirt left for a good battle. They got tired of Tater never staying dead like he was supposed to and Luther got sick of Captain Henry ordering him around. They kept arguing over who was boss, a captain or a general, and their Mammas kept telling them that they should be off reading or playing ball instead of partaking in such violent endeavors. So the game started to lose its excitement. But Captain Henry wasn't ready to let it go.

He was cleaning out Old Man Peterson's stables when he got the idea. Well, in all fairness, it was Chester the old horse snorting loudly in the next stall that gave it to him. Chester was so old he had near about outlived every member of Cedar Grove. And he looked it. He drooped. He sagged. He was like a broken down rusty old car left out in a deserted field that folks had grown so used to seeing that they don't notice it anymore. He was old, he was lazy, and he wanted nothing more out of this sweet life than to get dinner on time and occasionally have his chin rubbed. But that day Captain Henry saw something more than a crotchety old horse. He saw a fiery stallion. He saw nostrils flaring, mane flying in the wind. He saw a Captain charging into battle. It just about brought a tear to his eye. And so began his plan.

Word spread like wildfire among the kid folk that there was to be one final battle at the grounds of the new Post Office the following Saturday afternoon and the winner of the battle would be the winner of the entire war and would be king of Cedar Grove for all of eternity. This created quite a stir, because every kid wanted to be king. Even if they weren't sure exactly what that involved.

And when John Henry was cleaning out the attic like his mamma told him to, he found an old pair of black boots that had belonged to his Great-Grandpa. Do you think he saw a beat up old pair of galoshes with a rusty silver buckle? No sir, he saw spit-polished-till-they-shined black boots that belonged to a captain.

And when he found that rusted out old stock pot top with the handle, do you think he saw a beat up piece of junk? No sir, he saw a shield of honor. A captain's shield. Didn't matter to John Henry that it was a rather strange war having guns and shields and cannons and horses and generals and captains and kings — kind of mixed up if you was to study your history. But in the game of pretend war, you make up the rules as you go. Besides, John Henry didn't see all that. He saw the looks on their faces when he came charging in, the looks of awe as he was appointed King of Cedar Grove for all of eternity. He saw his name, "Captain Henry," being remembered forever.

Saturday was cool and sunny, the perfect day for a battle just as it was the perfect day for the grand opening ribbon cutting ceremony of the new Cedar Grove Post Office. A day that folks had been anticipating for months, especially Matilda May who was in charge of the entire ceremony, including polishing the fancy new horse statue that now stood covered by a red blanket waiting for its grand unveiling.

You could smell the fresh paint of the post office and there was a bright yellow ribbon tied to posts surrounding the statue where they had laid cement just fresh that morning. Women folk pulled out their fanciest bonnets and men donned their very best suspenders. Folks were proud.

But to the kids, it was an even bigger day. Not for some dumb ribbon cutting ceremony they knew nothing about but because it was the day of the final battle of Cedar Grove where every kid dreamed of becoming a king. They were gonna meet out front of the post office at a quarter till noon, which just so happened to be the very moment of the unveiling, a tiny detail John Henry was unaware of.

Captain Henry got up before the sun that morning in order to prepare for his grand arrival. Good thing, too, on account of getting Chester from the stables to the post office was not an easy task. Getting Chester to do anything was like catching a greased up pig — just near about can't be done. Chester hadn't walked that far in his whole life and by the time they arrived, he was wheezing and sputtering like a broke down car engine. It was amazing that no one caught sight of John Henry Jr. dragging that dilapidated old horse down the streets at dawn. But Captain Henry was determined. He would have carried that horse if'n he had to.

Now if you was to peer around back of the post office that morning, you would have seen John Henry in all his battle attire looking like the most lopsided, wrinkled, crumpled, moth-eaten, chewed up and spit out Captain that ever walked the face of the earth. But do you think he noticed it? No sir. He was a king. This was his moment. He had worked hard to make it happen. The hour was finally upon him.

He checked his watch and counted the seconds. He knew the others would be waiting around the corner and he would catch them in surprise. A quick fiery victory. His palms were sweating. *Ten. Nine. Eight.* He imagined all the great captains in history. *Seven. Six. Five.* Chester snorted. *Two. One...* "CHARGE," yelled John Henry as he kicked Chester's flanks. For once in that dilapidated old horse's life, he ran like the wind. Nostrils flaring, mane flying as they rounded the corner of the post office at the very moment that Matilda May was cutting the ribbon around the statue and pulling on the string to lower the blanket from the bronze horse.

"Charge," John Henry yelled again in the bold voice of a soon-to-be king and you can imagine his surprise when he saw what looked to be the entire town standing there before him with their jaws hanging wide open at the hinges. But nobody was more surprised than Chester, who in the middle of his once in a lifetime moment of glory, heard the firecrackers set off to celebrate the unveiling of the statue and caught sight of that giant bronze horse with its feet about ten feet above his head. That poor horse saw his entire life flash before his eyes and about had a heart attack right there on the spot.

"*N-n-n-e-e-i-i-g-g-h-h,*" he squealed and reared up on his hind legs, whereupon John Henry Junior slid right off his back like water off a duck while his trusty horse tore off down the street. And there lay John Henry Junior spread-eagled in the middle of that freshly laid cement beside the grand statue of Mayor Peabody in front of the new Cedar Grove Post Office.

There was a moment of silence and then the crowd roared, thinking it was all part of the entertainment, except for Matilda May, who was weeping uncontrollably because John Henry had ruined her grand opening, and Old Man Peterson who was running down the street after his horse, cursing John Henry from here to Wednesday, and John Henry's mamma whose nostrils were flaring bigger 'n Chester's. She let out one of her famous yells that could be heard three counties over and jerked

John Henry up by the ear and dragged him off down the street, yelling the whole way. Yes my friends, our Captain had been defeated. The brave gallant captain notoriously killed in battle. A fallen hero. What horror! What shame! But do you think that's what the townsfolk saw? No sir, they saw a troublemaking kid, wearing beat up old galoshes with a rusty silver buckle and pants three sizes too big, covered in wet cement from head to toe like he'd done bathed in oatmeal, leaving a soggy wet trail of footprints and dragging a rusty old stock pot top behind him.

He got a whupping that night, of course, and before too long he was into some other kind of trouble. But if you ever get a chance to get to Cedar Grove, go find that Post Office. It's not the biggest building in town anymore by far. But it's still there with the bronze statue sitting out front, more green than bronze. And beside that statue if you look down you will still see it. An imprint of a kid's body sprawled out like an angel print in the snow. All that's left to tell the story of John Henry Junior and the final battle of Cedar Grove.

And yes my friends, I do believe Captain Henry will be remembered forever.

The Time Nana Hawkins Almost Lost Her House

My mamma always said that God puts some people on this earth for the sole purpose of encouraging others. She said it may not sound like much, being an encourager, but that's like being the ocean underneath a cargo ship. Maybe it's the cargo ship that's carrying the important load but without that ocean, honey, it ain't never gonna leave the port. And whenever she'd bring up that particular analogy she was so proud of, she'd remind me of the time Nana Hawkins almost lost her house. Might not seem important to you but, to Nana Hawkins, losing that house was worse than the rapture happening thirty seconds before you was about to be saved. And Nana Hawkins was not known to exaggerate.

She'd grown up in that little yellow house with green shutters on the corner of Fourth and Maple, sandwiched in between Ray Jean's house and that old boarded up Peterson place, two doors down from Myrlene, Vyrlene, 'n Shirlene's House of Beauty. It wasn't a fancy house and, if I had to venture a guess, I'd say there were at least a gazillion houses just like it all over the world. But Nana Hawkins loved that house.

Not so much for the hardwood floors but for that one long board in the hallway that creaked every time you walked over it – third one in from the back. Some folks considered it a nuisance but not Nana. She considered herself immensely blessed having her very own built-in security system. It wasn't so much the wood stove built into the kitchen wall and surrounded by imitation brick that was considered quite the luxury in its day, but them initials scrawled at the base that told a story of another time.

It wasn't that cloudy old window that got stuck every time it rained but the fact that every time she opened it she'd be hit with a memory. A memory of kids playing kick the can in the street, that handsome mailman who always had a wink saved up just for her. Memories of her daddy leaned over the hood of his pick-up on a cool Saturday morning that smelled like honeysuckles. Oh, it was so much more than just a house.

It was built about a century back by a man named Sumner something, who sold it to his cousin Franklin something, who added on a deck, lived there ten years and then run off with his secretary and left the house to his wife, who lived in it a piece and ended up falling in love again and deciding that house had too many painful memories. So she sold it to Peter somebody, who lived in it for many years till he got run over by a milk truck and the house went to his eldest son Digger, who was Nana Hawkins's granddaddy. Only she wasn't called Nana then.

When Digger died from a gunshot inflicted during a dirty poker game, his estate was discovered to have been begotten by illegal means and was turned over to the state, which later sold it to Nana's daddy, Digger's son Buster, who'd gone off and made it rich in the plastics business and bought that house back so's it would stay in the Hawkins family. And he let his daughter Nana Hawkins (only she wasn't called Nana then) and her family live there for free, there not being any other siblings to argue over it, compliments of her daddy Buster. Bein' the cheap man that he was, he had them payments set up to stretch out over a fifty-year term. Only he died of pneumonia thirty years before the house was paid off and it was discovered about ten years later that this estate was also obtained by ill-gotten means, meaning Buster was a crook just like his daddy, just provin' that apple don't fall far from the tree, and the estate was rendered penniless. Or at least that's the way Mamma remembered it. She wasn't always so good with the details.

And Nana Hawkins, now called Nana, a widow with a grown daughter and a grandson to support, received a letter on official paper stating that she was now responsible for them payments or the house would be turned over to the state. Nana Hawkins didn't have the money. She was gonna lose the house. Word spread quicker than a turned-over pitcher of buttermilk that Nana Hawkins was in trouble.

Would have been simple if somebody could have stepped up and made them payments for Nana Hawkins. But in Cedar Grove things were never that simple. Times were tight and, while a hot plate of corned beef and cabbage for an oil change might have been considered a well-worth-it trade in Cedar Grove, it didn't work for house payments. But folks were determined to help out in any way they could. And as usual it was the womenfolk that reacted the quickest.

Phone lines burned up all over Cedar Grove clear into Buncombe County as womenfolk discussed their plan of action. A discussion which for the most part involved one percent planning and ninety-nine percent ruminating over the situation 'cause every good woman knows that a situation cannot be resolved until you have fully reviewed it from every angle, discussed it at great length along with any other relatively similar situations you have experienced or heard about, and traveled down the road of every *what if* you can possibly imagine so you will be prepared in the event that plans A, B, C, D, E, F, and G don't work and you have to resort to plan H, having decided that plan H will require another meeting in and of itself.

But the first step was abundantly clear as the women did the only thing they knew to do in a crisis of this nature. They started cooking. That was the 11th commandment in Cedar Grove: Ain't no situation on earth that can't be improved by a hot macaroni casserole. But this time baking casseroles wasn't gonna be enough.

Next step, put her on the prayer line 'cause it was also understood that there ain't no situation on earth can't be improved by running fervent prayer through an airtight chain of Baptist women. It wasn't thirty minutes before Nana Hawkins was the chief and primary concern of the Cedar Grove Baptist Church Prayer Line, and the Ladies Sewing Circle, and the Women on Missions group, the Gardenin' Club, the Welcoming Committee (they were slow on newcomers that month), and the Ladies Auxiliary, which was mighty impressive despite the fact that it was the same women who made up each group. Nobody had received this much attention since that time Booker Diggs's hound dog Grunt got stuck down in a well. Unfortunately, that story did not have a happy ending.

So Nana Hawkins sat in her beloved house knitting away her sorrows, surrounded by steaming casseroles and bundt cakes delivered in shifts by an assortment of blue-haired women with faces frozen in pity, intent on voicing their particular opinion about the situation at hand. A situation that went way beyond Nana Hawkins and her peer group, for it was like every woman in Cedar Grove felt an unexplainable tugging on her soul to help in whatever way she was able. It was like an unseen force was building with the strength of an approaching tornado. And like most tornados you don't want to be anywhere near its path, if you know what I mean. Frail men, stray dogs, little children run for cover. Lord help us, the women have joined forces.

It started with Fernetta Stutts, who ingeniously suggested a bake sale, to which they unanimously agreed 'cause if there was one thing that could draw a crowd in Cedar Grove, it was food. Grocery lists were made, ovens cranked up, and the sound of whirring mixers drifted out of every open window in town. Streets were covered with a fine dusting of sugar and flour for days. Aside from the one batch of fruitcakes that had to be thrown away 'cause Aunt Vyrnetta lost a cherry-red artificial fingernail somewhere in between the vanilla and the flour, it was unanimously agreed that the bake sale was a grand success, bringing in forty-four dollars and twenty-six cents.

"That's okay," said Mildred Jenkins. "The Lord will provide." Mildred had adopted the don't do nothing and let God handle it approach, which sounded good at first but, after years of hearing it, folks started looking elsewhere to find their pearls of wisdom.

"Mildred," said her sister Faye, "The Lord provides, but He don't say you got to roll over and play dead about it."

Ray Jean Jones offered up her diner as official campaign headquarters and the walls were soon covered with cross-stitched banners that said "Free Nana Hawkins" trimmed in lovely purple embroidered violets. Aunt Vyrnetta loaned Nana her very best wig straight out of her special occasion collection to wear to the meeting with the banker 'cause the way Aunt Vyrnetta saw it, ain't no tribulation in this world that's gonna excuse you from having bad hair.

"God don't care about your hair," said Mildred with her condescending smile. "He'll provide."

"Wish He'd provide a muzzle," muttered Aunt Vyrnetta. "So we can shut you up."

Aunt Bitsy jumped at the opportunity to share some of that useless knowledge she was always picking up off all those talk shows and infomercials by bringing Nana Hawkins articles on how to cope with stress — the latest technique involving straight pins, cooking oil, a girdle, and a tape of Elvis's Greatest Hits.

Granny Jean sold three of her wedding bands over at the *Pick and Pawn* and was even so kind as to offer Nana Hawkins a swig of that secret substance she kept hidden in the side pocket of her purse. It smelled like a dead animal and was rumored to literally grow hair on your chest. Nana Hawkins declined for obvious baptismal related reasons.

Porticia May Duberry offered to write a letter, 'cause, in Porticia's opinion, the very best way to register a grievance was to put it in the written word. She suggested that the letter be sent directly to the President himself and she had the address on file at home from the time she wrote him about the parking spaces out at the *Dollar Mart* being too close together. They all nodded in agreement. That was a good letter.

"Oh, Porticia," said Mildred. "You don't need a letter. God can hear your prayers. He'll provide." So Porticia did pray right there on the spot — for the patience to keep from punching Mildred Jenkins.

Norma Ray Peterson sewed arm bands so folks in Cedar Grove would feel a sense of unity. Besides, she had lots of black fabric left over from her daughter's clogging skirt that year she won first place in the State fair and did anybody need a copy of the newspaper article 'cause she still had a couple hundred left.

This triggered Vidal's decision to wear nothing but black till the situation was resolved, sort of a protest thing like one she saw on the TV news. Or was it one of them movies she saw on that women's channel? Vidal walked around town dressed head to toe in black looking like some kind of street mime. Folks weren't surprised. After all, she was from the city.

Aunt Bitsy asked did anyone want her to walk through the middle of town wearing her stringed bikini and white pumps like she did couple months back in that Conquerin' Fear story to which they quickly said no; they didn't think the town could survive another episode of that nature.

"Oh, Bitsy," said Mildred. "God doesn't expect theatrics. Lay your troubles at the feet of Jesus. You need to remember it is the Lord who provides." Aunt Bitsy then provided Mildred with a few choice words that ain't so appropriate for me to repeat in present company.

Eunice Simms, who played piano over at Cedar Grove Baptist, wrote a song about the whole endeavor 'cause she wrote a song about everything. The way she put it, ain't no situation in this world that don't become more touching when it is set to music. And as usual, her song ended up sounding suspiciously just like *Amazing Grace.*

Myrlene Smith organized a prayer vigil that would have made Moses proud, offering to donate one percent of all earnings from *Myrlene, Vyrlene, and Shirlene's House of Beauty* and then come up with the ingenious idea of holding the prayer vigil right there in the salon and letting all the ladies have their roots done for free in the process. She put a sign out front on her marquee that said, "Come root for Nana Hawkins. You come pray and we'll cover your gray." Myrlene was real good at that marketing.

Opal Henry come by on Mondays to help clean. Trudy sat with Nana on Tuesdays and they sewed and listened to *The Goodtime Gospel Greats* on the radio. Marge come by on Wednesdays to take Nana's mind off her troubles by sharing some troubles of her own, 'cause if there was one thing that woman knew how to do, it was share her troubles. If all else failed, she could always launch into the tale of her infamous gall bladder surgery, which always ended with a viewing of the scar.

Hester would come by on Saturday mornings with the latest letter from her daughter Mabel, who lived with her husband and kids over in the city and sent letters that were always sure to be filled with the sinful goings on of Mabel's children, the oldest of whom had just got caught wearing his Mamma's undergarments and what in heaven's name does a drag queen do? Is that anything like the Cedar Grove Sweet Potato Queen?

Emma Jean Maple set up a stand on the side of the road coming into town and sold pieces of colored glass, which folks couldn't really see the logic behind but that was Emma Jean Maple for you. And Mildred was always in the middle of it all saying, "The Lord will provide. The Lord will provide." Until she said it one time too many and Nana Hawkins took her knobby old wooden cane and sideswiped her upside the head and wasn't nobody who didn't think Mildred deserved it even when she started blubbering like an idiot, to which someone called out, "Oh Mildred, don't worry. The Lord will provide." And they all laughed.

Nana Hawkins, being the proud and humble woman she was, couldn't stand all this fuss and attention. But her words fell on deaf ears and big mouths. This had become so much bigger than Nana Hawkins.

"But why?" Nana Hawkins asked Fernetta Stutts. "Why are you putting yourselves out like this?" Fernetta Stutts stared at her like she'd grown a third eye, obviously not ever having given any thought to the question.

"Because," she told Nana Hawkins. "It's just what we do."

It happened at the beginning of the third week just as womenfolk were starting to run out of ideas. The situation was resolved. Just like that. No word or warning. Turns out the state got tired of women harrassin' them and calling and sending letters and photos of Nana Hawkins standing in front of her house, and more photos of little old ladies chaining themselves to trees. Tired of all the tapes titled "Ode to Nana's House" and the macaroni casseroles and bundt cakes delivered in shifts that was dangerously bordering on bribery, and some poor soul finally took it upon himself to mark that file PAID IN FULL. At least that's what the state claimed. Nobody ever really proved that's what happened. But it didn't matter. Wasn't nobody complaining. The situation had been resolved and every woman in Cedar Grove bathed in the glory of accomplishment.

Years later when all the details were fuzzy and the story's truth was stretched out as stories tend to get; when folks were claiming that Nana Hawkins almost suffered a stroke from the stress and that Porticia May Duberry actually spoke to the President; when folks couldn't really remember who started the prayer vigil or what color the arm bands were; when even Nana had trouble remembering whether it happened in the summer or in the spring. Even when Nana's own memory started to fade, there was one thing just as clear to her as if it happened yesterday. How all those women pulled together without giving it a second thought. Why? 'Cause that's just what we do. And ain't life just like that sometimes. Sometimes it ain't so much how the story ends but who was there to lift us up along the way. That's what matters. Well, that and good hair.

And Mildred, God bless her persistent soul. Nobody was there to see her in the quiet of her bedroom kneeling down in the moonlight with her silver head bent in prayer. Once again thanking her merciful Lord for providing. Just like she knew He would all along.

Maybe Mamma was right after all. Maybe God does put some people on this earth to encourage. How would we ever get by without them?

Callin' Earl

John Henry Junior, as you may already know, was a troublemaker. He didn't just get into trouble, he looked for it. And more times than not his trouble started with five little words. Five innocent-sounding words that never failed to lead John Henry Junior down the road to ruin: Wouldn't it be funny if... Wouldn't it be funny if he put soap bubbles in the fountain in front of Town Hall? Wouldn't it be funny to put Super Glue on Old Widow Jenkins's bicycle seat? Wouldn't it be funny if he dropped his pants and mooned the marching band? All were stunts that John Henry Junior only pulled once. Stunts that all started the same. Wouldn't it be funny if...

As everybody knows, in order for a true troublemaker to practice his craft there is one thing he must have when asking the question "wouldn't it be funny if" — a group of friends to answer "yeah, it would be funny if." John Henry was very blessed in that regard with his friends, Luther and Pete and Sam and Donald and Tater. He was never at a loss for a collective group of nodding heads.

Each kid in that group had his own special gift. John Henry was usually the planner of the group and the one who always tried to talk 'em all out of trouble somewhere at the end of the line. He could spit furthest and climb up a tree in no time at all barefooted.

Luther was the loyal friend and faithful follower – the kid you always wanted beside you when you headed into battle. He had the only autographed Hank Aaron rookie card in Cedar Grove and an endless supply of his Nana's fresh home baked chocolate chewy chunk cookies that could turn a boring rainy summer afternoon into a carnival of the senses.

Pete was tall and skinny and could squeeze through the fence in Old Man Jenkins' backyard when their baseball sailed over it. Sam wasn't afraid of danger. Whether it was wading through a swampy creek, jumping off the courthouse roof, or diving into home plate, he had no fear.

Donald drooled in his sleep — one of those gifts that can go either way, good or bad. Good, if you were in Pinkerton's math class when Donald set to dozing. Provided some great entertainment on many a boring hot afternoon. Bad, if you were at marching band camp with him and had to share a bunk. Donald was the voice of reason. The one who actually thought about the consequences of their actions and tried to see things from the adult perspective. Nobody ever listened to Donald.

And then you had Tater. That was his nickname of course, given to him on the day he was born when his daddy, who'd been "swimming in the spirits" as they used to call it in Cedar Grove, took one look at his newborn son, saw that big old bumpy bald head, belched loudly and said, "Honey, looks like you done give birth to a tater." He's been called that ever since.

Tater had the greatest gift a kid can ask for. A gift that was envied for miles around even clear over to Garnett County where his legendary name was whispered in awe. And oh what a beautiful gift it was. Not the gift of singing like a bird. Not the gift of running like a gazelle or painting like a Da Vinci. Tater had the one and only gift of its kind. Tater could barf at a moment's notice.

You know, throwing up, blowing chunks, calling Buicks, feeding the fish, gagging, heaving, launching your lunch, pavement pizza, retching, spewing spuds, slamming barf, tossing your cookies, upchucking, vomiting, retching, yakking, and my personal favorite, calling Earl – EEEEEAAARRRLLL.

Yeah, you heard me right. Tater could throw up on command. All you had to say was "Tater, we need us a barf" and he'd have one halfway up his throat 'fore you could even finish your sentence. Them barfs of Taters could work miracles. They could stop traffic. Guaranteed to get you out of a history test any day of the week. Them barfs could keep that other team from sliding into home plate and winning the game. It was beautiful and Tater was a hero.

Having a gift of such magnitude, however, had its price. Had its responsibilities. You couldn't do it too much 'cause one time too many and folks might start to suspect. So far they'd been successful 'cause, other than thinking Tater had a weak stomach, adults hadn't picked up on the fact that them kids were using that beloved barf technique to further their own personal agendas. There was only one time their barf technique was in serious jeopardy of being exposed. It was the Cedar Grove Middle School Spring has Sprung concert being held over at the Baptist Church that year 'cause the school's theater was getting painted and they didn't want their audience passing out or nothing.

The Spring Concert was like a talent show only without any talent. Kids would sing and dance, recite poetry, and do dramatic interpretations of famous people they'd been studying. Everybody had to be in the Spring Concert whether they had talent or not. One of those "everybody participates" kind of things like dodge ball that most kids dreaded. Except of course them kids that could play the fiddle or twirl the baton or clog or sing. They were just giddy with excitement. But not John Henry Junior. He was dreading it more than the flu shot, especially since Fernetta Stutts was making him and Luther and Sam and Pete and Donald be flowers. They had to wear these big old yellow and white daisy headpieces with green tights and a green leotard overneath.

John Henry told his Mamma that there wasn't no way he was wearing that costume and his Mamma said he would wear that costume and maybe it would teach him not to be so difficult in Miss Fernetta's class in the future. Yep, this was Fernetta Stutts's payback. And I must admit John Henry deserved it. So flowers they was.

Oh, but Tater, he didn't have to be a flower. Tater got to be a bird. He still had to wear tights but he got to wear black tights like Batman. And he got to wear this big set of giant wings strapped on his back and he could make whatever bird noise he wanted and he'd decided he was gonna make a noise like a crow — *caw, caw, caw.* And he got to run through the garden flapping his wings. John Henry just burned up with the injustice of it all.

Fernetta Stutts liked Tater best 'cause of that time he brought her a valentine. What a suckup Tater was. Only reason he did that was 'cause he found it in the hallway walking into class. Threw it on her desk 'cause he couldn't find the trash and she picked it up and turned all red and dabbed her eyes. Good grief. Now she liked Tater best. John Henry decided he was gonna get her back at all costs. It was the morning of the concert when he was sitting over his bowl of oatmeal and the idea hit him. Wouldn't it be funny if . . .

The boys met on the playground at break to discuss John Henry's idea which involved the concert, Fernetta Stutts, Tater, and his amazing barfing abilities. John Henry mapped out his Spewing Spring Concert Plan and all heads nodded in agreement. It was a good plan.

Like I told you, the concert was being held over in the sanctuary of the Baptist Church. Turns out that up front they had this brand new freshly filled up baptismal pool which sent Fernetta Stutts into a frenzied state of excitement 'cause one look and she knew that was gonna be the fountain for her spring garden. And all the flowers were gonna dance and sing around it and her bird was gonna fly in for a drink. She'd been talking about it for days she was so excited. John Henry and the others were excited too but for another reason entirely 'cause every time they pictured their plan they'd double over laughing.

The plan was that the flowers would sing and dance with great zeal and enthusiasm so as not to alert anyone of the upcoming prank. And then when it was time for the bird (i.e., Tater) to fly onto the scene for his drink in the fountain the boys would get ready. Tater was gonna fly around that fountain three times, cawing the whole time and then he was gonna caw three times in rapid succession — *caw, caw, caw* — and that was their cue, the cue for them daisies to back up ten paces and get ready for the barf that was soon to come. That cue was burned into their brains.

John Henry and the other boys didn't even mind practicing their spring song: *Spring, Spring, the world is green. All the birds and the flowers sing.* Didn't even mind putting on them green tights. It was worth it.

There was standing room only in the sanctuary that night with the mammas and daddies, cousins, grandmas and grandpas, cameras, videos, tape recorders, you name it. The Spring has Sprung concert was a big deal for a tiny town like Cedar Grove. Kids running all over the place... Little inch worms and willow trees. Little bumblebees with wings made out of panty hose stretched over coat hangers. A bunny with a polka-dotted bow tie. Looked like spring done exploded in that sanctuary.

Abigail twirled the baton in her pink leotard and white fish net tights and only dropped the baton twice. Charlie played Orange Blossom Special on the violin, or rather the one note version anyway. There were some dramatic interpretations and poems and soliloquies until finally it was time for them flowers to bloom from their bent over positions. John Henry and Luther and Donald and Sam and Pete were the best darn bloomers you've ever seen. They bloomed like they'd never bloomed before. There was barely a dry eye in the room. And Tater waited anxiously in the wings ready to go. Everything was falling right into place directly according to plan.

Unbeknownst to them there was an unseen force working against 'em that had started at lunch earlier that day when Tater made the mistake of ordering the mashed meat surprise. Mashed meat surprise was a combination of all the school cafeteria leftovers for that week. Peas, carrots, potatoes, hamburger, French fries. All mashed together to the consistency of a brick and covered in a warm lumpy gravy. I think Tater was the only one who ordered it that day 'cause the other choice was pizza and wasn't nobody gonna turn down pizza but Tater was allergic to cheese so he ate the mashed meat surprise. Didn't bother him none; he'd eat anything. Once he even ate a worm.

That mashed meat surprise sat in his stomach brewing like a slow simmerin' volcano, working up a hot lava that reached boiling point about four hours and twenty minutes later. Right in the middle of the Spring Concert. Two minutes before Tater could give his cue. For the first time in his life Tater had a barf coming up on him that was out of his control.

In a finely orchestrated plan of this nature a couple of minutes can make all the difference. A couple of minutes can be the difference in about four feet. A very important four feet. A couple of minutes can leave them daisies standing directly in the line of fire.

Just as Tater flew up to that baptismal pool where John Henry and the rest of them lovely flowers were singing their spring song, that volcano erupted. Before Tater had time to even fly around that fountain twice. Before he had time to give his cue. Before them daisies had time to clear the area.

Mashed meat surprise ain't that pretty going down. Coming back up is worse. Peas and carrots shot out Tater projectile fashion, followed by clumps of mashed meat surprise that hit the water of that baptismal pool with the force of bullets. If you've ever seen anybody do a cannonball off the diving board at the swimmin' pool you will know the effect them clumps of mashed meat surprise had upon hitting the water. Not so good for them daisies who suddenly found themselves singing and swimming in a spring shower of mashed meat surprise.

That volcano kept erupting and erupting, spewing lava over them daisies like dirt bikes through a mud puddle. Flowers went flying in all directions, arms flailing, feet flying. One daisy torpedoed through the air and into the choir loft. One sailed across the top of that piano. One daisy literally dove into a huddle of shivering bumblebees. It was pure pandemonium.

Fernetta Stutts was in the middle of it all, screaming like a military general. Fernetta Stutts did not like to lose control. In her eyes the show must go on despite the fact that her spring garden now looked like a family of squirrels done exploded in it. She started grabbing daisies hand over fist. Squinted up her eyes real tight and her face was so red and squinched up they thought her head might pop.

"Get up there and sing," she said between gritted teeth to them barf-speckled daisies. "And I'd better see every one of your lips moving or I will drown you in that baptismal pool myself." And she meant it too and them daisies scrambled back up on stage and within seconds were singing the praises of spring and the concert was back in session. *Spring, Spring, the world is green. All the birds and the flowers sing.*

After the show was over and the lights were back on and everyone had left except for them daisies who were lined up on the front row while the adults fired away question after question about the evening's endeavors. You see, the adults were suspicious; suspicious that an event of this nature could only have been planned. Suspicious that perhaps Tater had the ability to make himself regurgitate. The barf technique was in danger of being exposed.

At one point they thought Donald was gonna crack when his daddy got up in his face and threatened to cancel his yearly insect touring camping trip of Garnett County. But Donald held strong. As did they all. Held strong through the hours that followed and the whuppings and various punishments meant to break their code of silence. But they held strong. Because the barf technique was worth it. This was worth dying for.

After that they were more careful. They had paid a high price too. Learned a lesson they'd never forget. Not to call for a barf in the middle of a concert? No, to never let Tater eat the mashed meat surprise again.

Aunt Vyrnetta and Her One and Only Appearance on the Local News

Did I ever tell you about Aunt Vyrnetta and her one and only appearance on the local news? Well, Aunt Vyrnetta was one of those women you could say was consumed by her personal appearance. It was her favorite subject and she spent considerable time studying it. There wasn't a body part on that woman hadn't been tucked, sucked, plucked, tweezed, shifted, or lifted at one time or another. She wore these frighteningly long fingernails that curved at the tips and always (and I do mean always) matched her lipstick. She wore thick black false eyelashes, a beauty mole she done designed herself and wigs – a different one every day. Rumor had it that woman had a closet just for her hair and every one of them hairdos had a kick to it if you know what I mean 'cause Aunt Vyrnetta's thinking when it come to hair was that bigger was better. That woman was artificial from the inside out. Mamma used to say it was a shame she wasn't proud of the face God give her. Daddy said it was a wonder God even recognized that woman anymore at all. Might not have made a difference if Aunt Vyrnetta was a kind lady. But, well, she just spent too much time on herself to worry about other people, which is why this story is so blasted funny.

So how did she end up on the local news? Well, she was on the fundraising committee at the Cedar Grove Baptist church and was in charge of the entertainment for the annual fundraising dinner, where they usually got someone halfway famous to entertain and raise up some money. She figured she was the most important person she knew and decided it was in the church's best interest that she sing for the annual fundraising dinner – a sweet little number she'd just learned at voice lessons called *I Feel Pretty*. Cedar Grove didn't have a local news to speak of being such a small town and all but word got out to Garnett County and I guess they were short on news that week 'cause a reporter called up asking could he do a story on it. Well, being as Aunt Vyrnetta's husband was donating a hefty check to the church – ten percent of all used tire sales from the entire month – and seeing as how she was the one answered the phone when the reporter called, she elected herself to appear on the local news on behalf of the Cedar Grove Baptist Church. You can imagine what a project she made out of this. Just choosing the wig was a monumental decision in itself. Folks didn't see her for days. Not that they minded.

She made it known to everyone in town exactly what day and what time she was gonna be on the news and though most folks didn't exactly go out of their way to see Aunt Vyrnetta, well, it wasn't every day one of their own was on the TV. So every eye was watching her that night and good thing too 'cause no one would have believed it otherwise.

Aunt Vyrnetta was gonna be on after some bald man named Cyrus from over in Newchester who had him a parrot that could recite the Lord's Prayer. It was a really cool bird — real big and yellow with a wing span of about a foot. And Daisy (that was her name) sat up on Cyrus's shoulder and recited that entire Lord's Prayer complete with a bow at the end which we all agreed was a nice effect. Then the reporter ushered Cyrus and Daisy offstage and announced Cedar Grove's lovely Vyrnetta Henry and said how honored he was to have a small sampling of her talent for their show. Obviously he never heard her sing before. And then you heard this drumroll (no doubt Vyrnetta's idea) and out walked, no, out glided Aunt Vyrnetta, gussied up like she was about to meet the President.

It was all kind of corny, truth be known, her wearing this red shiny dress with sparkles on it (sequins I think they're called) that if you weren't careful would catch the light and blind you on occasion. She floated like a model, shaking her hips with that tiny smile, waving ever so slightly back and forth to all of us like she'd done just won Cedar Grove Sweet Potato Queen and was riding on her pageant float. She had on so much gold jewelry it was a wonder she didn't fall over. But it was her hair that beat all. The color she'd chosen was platinum, I think is what it was called. It was whiter than that fake snow they spray on the windows at Christmas. And it was piled way up high on her head, layer after layer, with tiny rolls all over it, made it look like a beehive it did. It was a work of art. Must have taken somebody weeks to put that thing together. Must have weighed five pounds all on its own. It's a wonder she could even hold her head up. I tell you what, that woman had outdone her very own self. And she knew it too as she stepped up to that microphone and got ready to sing.

It happened just as she sang the first note. It happened so fast that it's hard to remember the actual sequence of events, but first we heard this high pitched screeching noise coming from back stage and then something big and yellow flashed across the TV screen and it was like everything suddenly turned into slow motion. All heads turned to see those big wings flapping and feathers floating through the air belonging to none other than Daisy, the talking parrot, who seemed to be headed directly for Aunt Vyrnetta and picking up speed with every second. If'n you didn't know already, birds like things that glitter and shine. They're attracted to 'em. I'm guessing the sight of all that shimmer and gold and that platinum hairdo that just screamed out to be perched upon was just more than Daisy could take. And I kid you not, that giant wing-flappin' bird catapulted directly into Aunt Vyrnetta's platinum hairdo with a huge thud and latched its thick claws into her platinum beehive wig and looked at us like it was just the most natural perching spot in the world.

Only I guess Daisy wasn't figuring on the reaction she would get from Aunt Vyrnetta who completely came undone like a crazy woman and let out a blood-curdling scream and started jumping up and down and batting at her head trying to knock that bird off and screaming, "Get it off me, get it off me, get it off me." And I don't rightly blame her, I would have been the same way too if'n I had a talking bird on my head, wouldn't you?

Well this scared poor Daisy silly and she couldn't have gotten loose if she wanted to 'cause her big old thick gray claws were tangled up in that platinum beehive hairdo something fierce and she kept flapping her gigantic wings squawking over and over, "Get it off me, get it off me, get it off me." And I don't rightly blame her, I think I would have been the same way if'n I was that up close to Aunt Vyrnetta, wouldn't you?

Vyrnetta kept screaming and jumping around and Daisy kept squawking and I don't know who was cursing worse, Aunt Vyrnetta, or that talking bird that let out a string of obscenities that liked to make a sailor blush. All you saw was a blur of sequins and feathers. And the reporter just stood there with his mouth hanging open just like the rest of the folks back home. It was the best news story we'd ever seen in our lives.

Finally Cyrus ran on stage and tried to pull that bird off Aunt Vyrnetta's head, only that wasn't such an easy task 'cause those claws were tangled something fierce and Aunt Vyrnetta was screaming and Daisy was squawking and Cyrus was pulling and pulling until finally he pulled off her head. Well, that's what it looked like anyway. He really pulled off the wig and he's standing there holding Daisy, who's holding the wig, and Aunt Vyrnetta's standing there to the side with this horrified look on her face realizing she was still on the TV. With good reason too if you could have seen her.

She was lopsided because one heel had broken off her shoe. Her sparkly dress was all bunched up around her hips and her panty hose had rips and tears all over 'em. Gold jewelry was scattered all over the floor, mixed in with a couple of fake fingernails. Her lipstick was smeared up one side of her face and that beauty mole she'd done designed herself was now plastered to the side of her nose and a big old fake eyelash hung from her cheek like a spider. But that wasn't the worst part. The worst part was that pantyhose stocking looking thing she had on her head I guess to hold the hair in place underneath where that wig used to be. Looked like she was about to rob the place. The *I Feel Pretty* music still played softly in the background. And that was the last sight we saw before they cut to a commercial.

Folks in Cedar Grove just sat there staring at each other, not even able to put words to what they just saw. And then someone somewhere let out a giggle, followed by another, and another, until folks were rolling on the floor laughing in every house in Cedar Grove. They laughed till tears streamed out of their eyes. They laughed till they felt their sides were splitting. They laughed so hard it was like one giant cloud of laughter rose right up in the sky and directly into God's ear and I do believe He was laughing too. And next time they saw Aunt Vyrnetta they laughed all over again. To this day it will bring a chuckle to anyone who remembers Aunt Vyrnetta and her one (and only) appearance on the Local News.

Iced Tea

John Henry Junior was a troublemaker, but you have to admit that it's not always easy being a kid. Somebody always telling you to sit down, act your age, grow up. He heard that all the time and figured that when you got to be an adult that you automatically knew how to act like one. At least that's what he used to think, until that family reunion when his grandmother Beatrice was still alive.

Mammy Bee was eighty-years-old that year and no taller than a full-grown pony with frizzy black hair that shot out of her head in all directions like static electricity. She was crazy and I don't mean just a little nutty. She was deep down, to the soul, one-card-short-of-a-deck kind of crazy. She had what adult folk in the family referred to as "Old Timer's" disease, which is kind of like amnesia only you don't have to fall on your head to get it. John Henry chose a spot near her 'cause he hated family reunions and she was just about the closest thing to entertainment as he was gonna find. And that's how he happened to witness the whole incident. Otherwise, he wouldn't have believed it. It all started over a simple glass of iced tea.

Only people in the room 'sides John Henry were Mammy Bee and Aunt Vyrnetta. Aunt Vyrnetta was the kind of woman you could say was consumed with her personal appearance. It was her favorite subject and she spent considerable time studying it. And that woman was about as artificial on the inside as she was on the outside and didn't have much patience for Mammy Bee. Mammy Bee didn't like Aunt Vyrnetta either even on days she didn't recognize her. Aunt Vyrnetta changed her hair color more often than a person changes underwear which just added to Mammy's confusion. That year it was a red color that was so bright you couldn't look at it for too long or your eyes would hurt, kind of like looking into the sun. She called it cherry-blossom special but bush on fire would have been a better name. Anyway, Mammy Bee had somehow talked Aunt Vyrnetta into getting her a glass of iced tea.

"Here you go, here's your tea," Aunt Vyrnetta shouted at Mammy Bee. She obviously thought having "Old Timers" meant you were deaf too. "Now drink up." She patted Mammy on the head. Mammy Bee held the glass up to the light and inspected it.

"This tea's kind of cloudy," she said with a puzzled expression. "And this ain't the right glass. This is my juice glass. I drink tea out of the glass with the yellow daisies on it. Can't drink tea out of this glass. Run and go get me my daisy glass," Mammy said flashing her best I'm-a sweet-little-old-lady-and-aren't-I-just-precious smile. It was wasted on Aunt Vyrnetta who grabbed the glass (quite harshly) and stormed off to the kitchen, her high heels clip-clopping furiously down the hallway. She returned with the proper glass.

"Here you go, the glass with daisies on it," Aunt Vyrnetta said, though not as sweetly as before. "Now drink it up before it gets warm." She tried to escape but Mammy was quicker.

"This tea ain't got any ice cubes in it," Mammy Bee exclaimed in horror. "Drink just ain't a thirst-quenching drink 'lessin it's got ice in it, as my Joshua used to say. Run back in and get me some ice for my tea. Why I declare..." said Mammy, muttering something under her breath John Henry couldn't make out. Vyrnetta hesitated then gritted her teeth and grabbed that glass with white knuckles and a look that said she'd rather pour that tea on Mammy's head.

When they could hear those heels clip-clopping angrily down the hallway Mammy looked over at John Henry and just as simple as you please, winked. That's right. Just a small crazy woman wink, but it said so much. The way John Henry figured it Mammy wasn't crazy as she let on and she was using her condition to get away with things she otherwise wouldn't get away with. Terrorizing Aunt Vyrnetta was probably the last bit of sunshine left in that lonely old woman's life and she was determined to make the best of it.

"Mammy Bee, your secret is safe with me," thought John Henry as Aunt Vyrnetta returned.

"Here you go, now drink your tea," Aunt Vyrnetta ordered practically throwing the glass at Mammy Bee, no longer even trying to be nice. John Henry figured he probably would have quit right there but it appeared Mammy was just getting started.

She slurped her tea loudly, sticking out her pinky finger like she was royalty. Just as Aunt Vyrnetta got to the doorway Mammy started spitting dramatically, clutching her chest, and spewing iced tea out of her mouth like a busted dam. John Henry stared in awe.

"This tea ain't sweetened," Mammy yelled, her face twisted and contorted like she just bit into a ripe lemon. "Tastes like I'm sucking on a wet sponge! Where'd you learn how to make tea? The city dump?" Aunt Vyrnetta froze in the doorway and turned around slowly with a calm look on her face. She walked over to Mammy Bee just as slow and leisurely as a Sunday walk in the park and leaned over her chair close enough for Mammy to smell her breath.

"I am trying to be patient with you, old woman," she said through clenched teeth. John Henry strained to catch every word. "I am not your maid and you will not order me around. I got you your tea. I put it in the glass with the daisies on it. I added the ice cubes. Now shut up and drink your @*!#$ tea, you old bat!" John Henry's jaw dropped. Cursing in Mammy Bee's house was unthinkable not to mention calling her a bat.

"Don't you speak to me like that in my own home," said Mammy Bee with nostrils flaring. *Good-bye, sweet little old lady.* "This is a fine southern home. And while you don't even have an ounce of lady in you, you will have the decency to act like one under my roof." Way to go, Granny. And that's when Aunt Vyrnetta, having obviously run out of verbal insults, did what any rational adult woman would do under the circumstances. She stuck out her tongue. John Henry wondered exactly who in that room was crazy.

"How dare you stick your tongue out at me," Mammy said. "Why I've a good mind to whup that flabby butt of yours right here and now. Coming into my home and disrespecting me that way. You over-painted hussy!" John Henry's jaw dropped.

Aunt Vyrnetta's face reflected her internal turmoil as she was obviously debating the smart thing to do, which was to walk away, or the tempting thing to do, which was to kill Mammy Bee. And then Aunt Vyrnetta did what all of 'em had been itching to do at one time or another but had never dared. She raised her finely-manicured freshly-polished hand and belted Mammy Bee upside the head. John Henry's heart actually skipped a beat.

They stared at each other and John Henry stared at them. He felt like the commentator of a boxing match watching that crucial opening moment when the two athletes stand together face to face their eyes locked in a challenge much deeper than the physical one to follow. Mammy's primeval scream ripped through the air and she lunged at Aunt Vyrnetta's fire engine red hair, latching on as if her very life depended on it. And things got cloudy after that as the two women commenced to scrapping.

And they're off, ladies and gentlemen. Mammy Bee opens up with a right hook to the jaw. Aunt Vyrnetta reels backwards in surprise, catches her breath, and leaps at Mammy Bee's head with a hold never before seen in professional wrestling. It was hard to tell who was winning on account of they had melted into this mass of flailing body parts screaming and hollering like she-cats in an alley. John Henry saw elbows and feet, brassieres and girdles, bunions and moles. Fake plastic fingernails shot out of the fray like bullets. He saw a flash of a thigh, a hint of a stomach, and a couple of body parts he'd have rather not seen if it were his choosing. He dodged a red high-heeled torpedo hurling towards him at lightning speed and narrowly missing his head. Mammy's dentures shot out of the fray and landed on the floor at his feet in a smile. He heard a high-pitched squeal as Mammy's orthopedic shoe made contact with Aunt Vyrnetta's flabby butt. Ten points for Mammy Bee, who it seems has taken the lead. Ladies and gentlemen, your money was well spent tonight. Could it be? Yes! I can't believe it, folks, in front of our very eyes. Mammy Bee has gone for the hair.

No TV show could have been more exciting than watching Mammy Bee hang on to Aunt Vyrnetta's cherry-blossom special until she pulled it off, revealing Vyrnetta's real hair which was black and short and all smooshed down on her head by what looked to be pantyhose. Aunt Vyrnetta froze in horror. She looked like a criminal on Most Wanted. Even Mammy Bee took a step back and blinked her eyes, not sure what to make of this strange overly madeup woman with her head shoved into a nylon stocking. Both of 'em panted heavily. Mammy's knee-highs were puddled at her ankles and her broken spectacles were hanging off of one ear. It was a sight John Henry would remember forever.

And just when he was waiting for the bell to signal round two, the others came running into the room, spoiling the entire moment as only adult folk can do. And they all start carrying on and pointing fingers. And before they knew it Mammy and Vyrnetta were at it again and it took three men to pull them apart. John Henry's daddy raised his hand and when everybody finally stopped talking at once, he asked for an explanation.

Mammy Bee's chin quivered and her head dropped. Her eyes puddled up with tears and in the sweetest, tiniest voice like a five-year old, she answered, "All I did was ask for a glass of iced tea."

After that whenever anybody told him to act his own age or to grow up, John Henry would remember his Mammy Bee and her glass of iced tea.

That Conquerin' Fear Idear

Aunt Bitsy was a large woman by anyone's definition and a walking sponge of information — useless information for the most part, picked up in places like the drugstore or the beauty parlor. 'Cause everybody knows information obtained while you're getting your roots done is sacred and not to be questioned. Aunt Bitsy was always looking for a cause, usually one picked up off an afternoon talk show, also the most trusted of sources. Like the time she became a vegetarian after a particularly moving episode about the emotional impact of animals being led to slaughter. That lasted about two weeks when she quickly lost interest and became involved with one of them spirit of the world churches and started wearing earrings with moons on 'em and skirts made out of kelp. Still ain't really sure what kelp is.

The church asked her to sell all her belongings, donate 'em to the church, and move into a tent on the outskirts of town. Aunt Bitsy couldn't see where her weekly waxin's and facials over at *Myrlene, Vyrlene, and Shirlene's House of Beauty* was gonna fit into that whole equation, so she give it up. The church I mean, not the salon. Shoot, she wasn't stupid.

Then she launched on a quest to adopt a little Cambodian youngun like she saw on one of them infomercials. Learned a very painful lesson in that process: how it ain't always a good idea to try and order you a youngun off of the Internet. Luckily, no one pressed any charges.

Aunt Bitsy heard this highfalutin' head doctor give a talk on conquering your fears. The way this doctor explained it, if you were afraid of something like heights, or dogs, or water, then the best way to cure it was to do the very thing you were afraid of. So I'm guessing if you're afraid of snakes you're supposed to crawl into a bathtub full of them thick slimy angry hissing creatures. Well, I suppose he was right, guess your fears would be conquered 'cause you'd be dead. I don't think so. Like to see that highfalutin' head doctor do it first. Anyway, it don't matter what I think, 'cause Aunt Bitsy took it all to heart and got it into her head that it was high time she conquered some fears of her own, starting with her fear of wearing a bikini.

Yes, Aunt Bitsy was afraid of wearing bikinis and hadn't worn one in, well, never. I don't mean to sound disrespectful but the way I saw it, that woman had every reason to be afraid. So Aunt Bitsy gets it into her head that she is gonna conquer her fear and conquer it but good. And the proper way to do this would be to walk directly through the center of town wearing nothing but a bright yellow string bikini and white pumps. No skirt, no cute wraparound, no muumuu covered in tropical flowers, we are talking full exposure. And not in the morning before everybody was up or late at night after everybody turned in, but right there in the middle of lunch hour, busiest time of day in Cedar Grove. And down Main Street, busiest street in Cedar Grove. And by God, Aunt Bitsy did it.

She didn't cower. She didn't walk hunched over. She marched. She marched right past Ray Jean's diner and that big bay window where all them forks sat frozen in mid-air. She marched right past the high school where her son Donald (third row trumpet) was having band practice and undergoing the most excruciatingly painful experience in his life. She marched like a woman on a mission because the way she saw it, she was paving the way for every other woman to come after her. Her vision was grand but I ain't so sure she accomplished her goal.

In all the excitement of the event Aunt Bitsy never realized the full implications of purchasing something known as a thong bikini. Shoot, she thought thong just meant it was made somewheres in China or something. Wearing a bikini through the center of town was one thing. Wearing a thong bikini was something else. Talk about making a statement. And it don't stop there. Aunt Bitsy, on a last minute whim, charged up by all the applause and adrenalin, added some dance steps to her little number. Problem was, the only dancin' she knew about was clogging, and, for future reference, clogging ain't the type of dance you should pick when wearing a string bikini and white pumps. There were parts of that woman exposed that only God Himself knew about. And each part was taking on a very life of its own, shaking and shimmering to the beating rhythm of them marching pumps like one of them country choirs where every person is struggling to be the solo. News spread quicker than chicken pox through a daycare.

Fernetta Stutts, math teacher over at the elementary school, pitched a fit when Aunt Bitsy marched past her window full of second graders learning fractions, claiming there were some things weren't fitting for a youngun to see, and why didn't they hire that school guidance counselor way back when she suggested it 'cause these younguns were gonna need some of that psychiatric treatment to keep them from being scarred for life.

Beauregard DuBerry was all in an uproar 'cause now his wife wanted to walk through town wearing her string bikini, which he felt just wasn't appropriate what with her running for city council and all.

Ray Jean complained that her food sales went down 10%, and wasn't a thing wrong with her corned beef and cabbage. A group of folks started picketing Aunt Bitsy, saying she was making fun of the weight challenged and then a group started picketing the picketers (it was big that year) saying it was those weight challenged people that Aunt Bitsy was sticking up for.

And then there were those who thought it wasn't Christian what Aunt Bitsy was doing, to which others replied wasn't nowhere in the Bible did it state that God had an aversion to thong bikinis. And the mayor kept pleading with Aunt Bitsy to take her business back home, asking what would happen if they all started marching around wearing nothing but string bikinis and white pumps, to which someone replied maybe the town might just be a better place for it.

And then there were some who, underneath all the *I can't believes*, and *How could she's*, and *Who would ever's*, had this tiny voice saying *You go, girl* and thinking that if we all had a little bit of Aunt Bitsy in us, maybe this world might just be a little better off for it. But who am I to say?

Aunt Bitsy was given a citation for indecent exposure in public and her picture was plastered on the front page of the paper and the local news and everybody knows the camera adds ten pounds, which didn't do much to further her cause. And, well, I'm still not sure if she got the result she was aiming for. But I do know this; they sold out of bikinis in every department store within fifty miles that year. All sizes, even plus sizes. And there's some that's giving Aunt Bitsy the credit.

And then Myrlene Smith decided to conquer her fear of treadmills and Horace Peabody decided to conquer his fear of drowning and Old Man Jenkins figured it was high time he got over his fear of heights and that's when things started to spiral out of control. But I'm afraid that's another story.

Cornmeal in the Collection Plate
(The story of how Pastor Isaiah lost his spirit)

Did I ever tell you the story of the time Pastor Isaiah lost his spirit? Oh, I don't mean that he took a trip over to the dark side, or even that he stopped believing, nothing as serious as that. He just hit a period of deflating, like a month-old balloon left over from the state fair.

Isaiah was a natural-born pastor with a passion for the Lord that just ate him up. As a kid, he preached on the playground, in the classroom, at the bus stop. He preached in the grocery store lines and in the waiting room at the doctor's office. He once even preached on the corner of Fourth and Maple when Cleetus Harley's cousin Bo moved to town and tried to start one of them establishments where women walked around in their unmentionables. Stood on that corner for three days straight.

There was no doubting his devotion to the Lord and him becoming Pastor was as natural to the folks of Cedar Grove as a bear doing his business in the woods, if you'll excuse the expression. And he spent most of his days and nights fervently praying for his flock and seeking God's purpose in his life. But sometimes even Pastors need help 'cause after all they are only human, and it would do most of us good if we remembered that from time to time. Thing was, nobody saw it coming and was hard for folks to understand in a tiny town that didn't like strangers, didn't like change, and most definitely didn't like it when they couldn't see things coming.

It happened after that paper mill closed down in Garnett County, sending most folks in Cedar Grove straight down the road to hard times. Everybody felt it that year, including the collection plate over at the Cedar Grove Baptist Church, which worried them deacons something fierce 'cause they weren't just in the red, they had to look way up to even see the red. But Pastor Isaiah assured them everything would work out and figured up a budget that would have made the federal government proud. And he wrote a sermon that would have made old Mr. Scrooge himself empty out his pockets right there on the spot. But the collections got smaller and the bills got bigger.

So he stayed up later, pored over every Biblical resource he owned, and wrote another sermon that he was sure would change folks' minds about the whole tithing issue. And when he delivered it he used every public speaking tip he could get his hands on, from deep rooted eye contact to the spontaneous tear rolling down the cheek. And the collections got smaller.

Finally, Pastor Isaiah began to worry. He talked to God about it but, for the first time in his life, he felt like God wasn't answering. And Pastor Isaiah took this very personally and I guess you could say that's when his sinful side reared its ugly head and can't none of us say we don't know the feeling. And come the following Sunday morning, Pastor Isaiah woke up and decided he didn't feel like preaching anymore.

You can imagine what a shock it would be to the folks in that tiny town who built their security on certain things like the Sweet Potato Festival always being the weekend before Thanksgiving, Cleetus Harley's pot-bellied pig always winning first prize at the state fair, Aunt Marge's gall bladder surgery story always ending with a viewing of the scar, and the preacher showing up on Sunday morning. They didn't ask for much in Cedar Grove so you can imagine their surprise that Sunday morning when the pulpit was empty.

Folks sat there looking at each other at first, wondering if there was a time change, or if maybe Pastor Isaiah was running late again like that time he almost missed his sermon cause them clips got stuck on his baptismal suspenders.

Eunice Simms, who played the organ, kept repeating the opening hymn, "Amazing Grace," which is a beautiful song until you get to the thirty-third playing of it and the choir didn't really know where to go with it after all the verses ended so folks just started singing however the Spirit led 'em, which wasn't really a joyful noise unto the Lord, but rather quite painful to the ear except to those who had their hearing aids turned down. I'm sure anyone passing outside the church at that moment came up with some new conclusions about Baptists.

Hank Butrell kept rearranging the collection plates trying to look all official, being head deacon and all, a title he bestowed upon himself 'cause he'd been there the longest and was the only one outside the pastor who had keys to the fellowship hall. A couple of folks sat there fervently praying, including little old widow Jenkins who was convinced that the rapture had done happened and she was left behind with all the rest of them heathens. And finally an uncomfortable quiet fell on the congregation as folks settled into the fact that Pastor Isaiah had stood them up. For the first Sunday in the history of Cedar Grove there was no sermon, and folks went home burdened with a strong sense of guilt and an even stronger sense of urgency to spread the news to those who had not witnessed it firsthand.

Folks weren't sure how to handle the situation, as it didn't seem to fall into the usual categories like a wedding or a funeral or a woman whose husband has just run off with his secretary. So the women did what they usually did – started cooking — 'cause ain't no situation can't benefit from a good hot macaroni casserole. And wasn't a woman in Cedar Grove who didn't have that phone glued to her ear in the process.

The menfolk did what they did best, which was to coordinate an investigation in hopes of assessing and therefore correcting the situation. And a group of 'em headed over to Pastor Isaiah's house, some carrying shotguns in case there was some kind of criminal-like activity involved, Harvey Diggs leading the pack, what with him being a veteran and all.

The kidfolk did what they did best, which was to follow along unnoticed hoping to get to see their first real live dead body up close or at least get away with something while their parents were otherwise distracted.

Pastor Isaiah didn't answer the door, which put them menfolk on a heightened sense of alert and gave 'em one of them Audie Murphy kind of experiences. After much discussion on whether it would be better to break through the front door, leaving the house exposed to the elements (and it was supposed to rain later that evening), or whether it was better to break into a back window, knowin' full well that it takes three weeks to get glass ordered from Garnett County and was a dead body really worth the wait. Someone finally had the sense to turn the door knob to find the door was unlocked, a common occurrence in

Cedar Grove and something they would have known had they not been in all swept up in that Audie Murphy thing.

They charged into the Pastor's house like they was on some kind of SWAT team while younguns peered in from every available window like critters looking for food. And imagine their surprise when they found Pastor Isaiah sitting there in his easy chair still in his bathrobe with three days growth on his chin looking at them like he was seein' them for the first time and then turning back to watch the TV set which wasn't even turned on.

The menfolk did what they did best and just sat there without saying a word and then left him to his peace to sort things out on his own.

Of course the womenfolk were not too pleased when these men come home with no information. After all, some of us women just thrive on the details. And since folks didn't have any answers they started coming to their own conclusions as to the current state of their beloved Pastor.

Some said it was the feud between the Peabodys and the Chesterfields that had gone on for so long nobody could remember how it started, including the Peabodys and the Chesterfields. And poor Pastor Isaiah was always caught in the middle. Others said it was the Joneses moving three counties over to start their own religion that encouraged free love. Said that like to have broken the poor Pastor's heart. Some thought it was all them empty altar calls and the fact that there wasn't anybody left in town who Pastor Isaiah hadn't already witnessed to. And then you had those like Aunt Bitsy, who swore it had something to do with that dreaded Sweet 'n Low that she'd been swearing for years was eventually gonna kill us all.

But the popular rumor that turned into truth in their minds anyway was that Pastor Isaiah was giving up his calling and the church was in financial difficulty 'cause folks weren't tithing their 10% — a very sore subject in a tiny town where 10% to some meant the difference 'tween one helping or two.

Not only did Pastor not feel like preaching but also didn't feel like bathing, or shaving, or taking out the trash, or even making himself presentable to the assembly line of ladies who brought casseroles over in shifts. Or the choir who came to sing his favorite hymns. Or Booker Diggs, who came to play the jaw harp in hopes of pulling Pastor out of his state of depression. The following Sunday rolled around and Pastor still refused to leave his chair and he was starting to look like a pair of chewed up pantyhose that's done had a bad experience with the spin cycle and folks was starting to worry about him getting bedsores and wondering should they start turning him or something.

Hank Butrell preached the sermon the following Sunday, him being head deacon, and taught a valuable lesson in why God calls some folks and not others. The sick weren't getting visited and the homeless weren't getting meals. It was pitiful and the town was on high alert. The story wasn't so new anymore and folks were ready for things to go back to normal. Finally, they did what they should have been doing all along. Praying. Well, it was about time is what I say. And people started praying like they'd never prayed before.

In all the chaos nobody even noticed that family passing through town. Porter, I think was the name, and they barely had enough money to pay for a room at Ray Jean's. Ray Jean rented out a room behind the diner and she gave 'em a deal what with it being her off season of course, off season meaning the room wasn't occupied for the moment.

The Porters were dirt farmers, which is what folks in Cedar Grove called those rare few that were even poorer than themselves. Being church-going people, the Porters set out to find somewhere to worship, which didn't take long seeing that there was only one church in Cedar Grove, the Baptist Church, and the next closest church was driving distance and it was rumored to be one of them spirit of the world churches that encouraged free thought and expression, at least that's what folks in Cedar Grove had heard, so the Porters decided the Baptist church it would be, despite the rumors that it was currently running on a wing and a prayer.

It was Aunt Bitsy who finally had an idea that made some sense for a change, when she mentioned that she saw on one of them afternoon talk shows where they was discussing this technique to bring folks out of the pits of sorrow – something called an intervention. Kind of like tough love, where the family all gets together and talks some sense into the individual. Cedar

Grove figured it didn't need no fancy word like intervention. Shoot, they'd been talking sense into folks for years.

So they called up Pastor Isaiah's brother the Colonel who arrived in Cedar Grove not even twenty-four hours later, which just furthered their faith in the military. The Colonel had changed since they'd last seen him. For starters, he was a Colonel now and was just about as big and intimidating and military looking as a person can be. Haircut real close to his head, a build that clear filled out a doorway, and a booming voice that could immediately train a wild wolf and said this man don't take no junk from nobody. Colonel jerked Pastor Isaiah up off of that sofa, threw him in the shower and announced to the current shift of well wishers and casserole bakers that Pastor Isaiah would be in the pulpit the next morning, spit-polished and shining like brass. And folks believed him, 'cause after all, some of 'em had known him since the day he was born.

Don't know exactly what happened behind closed doors but Colonel was true to his word and Pastor Isaiah was standing there at the pulpit next morning and the sanctuary was filled to the rafters from the front row where that Colonel sat stiff and straight as an ironing board, all the way to the back row where that Porter family was sitting quietly in their dirty overalls and scrubbed up faces.

Pastor gave his sermon, one he did a couple years back. He said all the right words, looked up at all the right places, and paused at all the right moments. But something was missing. He knew it. The congregation knew it. And I suspect the Lord knew it too.

But folks were still happy to have their Pastor back and order restored to their town so they could get back to more important business like the current rumor that Myrlene, Vyrlene, and Shirlene Smith had all made appointments over in Garnett County to have their noses reconstructed to look like Sandra Dee's.

And after everybody was gone, Pastor Isaiah sat in his empty office, surrounded by the collection plates and left over casseroles, staring out the window feeling empty and lost as a stray pup left out on the side of a dark highway. He watched folks going on about their business and noticed that new family walking off by themselves. He hadn't even bothered introducing himself and felt a twinge of shame knowing that was the only sermon they would hear from him and it had been pitiful 'cause a sermon without the Lord in it is like a brand new hot rod convertible with no engine. Oh it may look pretty, but without that engine you ain't never gonna get out of the driveway.

Pastor Isaiah sighed and started counting the collection money with a heavy heart that was asking God for some meaning to all of this. And in the quiet of that afternoon God finally answered.

Pastor picked up the last collection plate and stared at it with a puzzled expression 'cause laying there among the crumpled up bills and change was a dirty white bag tied up with string. The bag didn't hold coins or bills but a yellow substance like sand. The Pastor poured it through his fingers, smelled it, and realized it was cornmeal, of all things. Someone had put cornmeal in the collection plate. But who? And why?

He'd known these people for years and they'd never done anything like this before. It just didn't make sense. And then he remembered the last row, near the door, in the dirty overalls and scrubbed up faces. What was their name? He couldn't remember. But it didn't matter what their name was. What mattered was the fact that those dirt farmers had given cornmeal as their tithe. He was sure of it.

Give back unto the Lord, the Pastor had told his people over and over through the years. *Give with a joyful spirit. The best of what we have belongs to the Lord. The first of what we have belongs to the Lord. All that we have belongs to the Lord.* God was speaking to Pastor Isaiah.

And God was sending him a message. A message in a little white bag tied up with string and delivered by a stranger. A stranger who, when faced with nothing to give, gave all he had. And the Pastor felt the shame of a truth that can hit you like a splash of cold water.

Isaiah felt that burden being lifted off him as he began to write the next week's sermon. He called it "Cornmeal in the Collection Plate."

Fender Fella and the Dairy Princess
A Love Story

Ya'll remember that ever-so-popular story about Cinderella and them three ugly hairy stepsisters and that stepmamma who was as mean and nasty as a coon caught up in a trap? Mighty fine fairy tale if I ever heard one. Well, you ain't gonna believe this, but Cedar Grove's got a story just like that. Okay, some of the details may be a tad bit askew, but there ain't no denying the resemblance. You could say it's a Cedar Grove Fairy Tale.

Cedar Grove was a tiny town about a mile and a hair past nowhere. They had two stoplights total, an old brick schoolhouse that also served as the town hall and bingo headquarters on Thursdays. Of course they didn't play for real money what with it being a town built around a Baptist church and all. They were mighty proud of their one-half of a fast food restaurant. The other half was technically in Butner.

We all know that in fairy tales you got to have a princess and this fairy tale's got one good as any. But the story isn't really about the princess. It's about the prince. But like most things in life it took a woman to get the whole thing started, which brings me to the beginning of my story and the day Vidal made her entrance into Cedar Grove. Now, in case you're a little slow in picking up on things, Vidal is our beloved and enchanted Fairy Godmother. She probably ain't what first comes to mind when you think of Fairy Godmothers but then even the Fairy Godmother Association understands about equal opportunities for all, including a bony, scatterbrained, busy-bodied, black-haired pasty-faced palm-reader straight off the streets of New York.

Folks didn't trust her from the start cause she only had one name and all. Now we're used to that today what with the likes of Cher, and Prince, and Barney, but folks in Cedar Grove weren't accustomed to the concept and just found it plain weird. I mean whoever heard of a name like Vidal? Not Vydal, or Videlle, or Vidalia, but Vidaaaaaaaaal. A name that nobody in Cedar Grove could even say with a straight face. Little secret between you and me, Vidal got her name off of one of them bottles of hairspray when she was wandering through the SuperMart but we won't tell nobody. Nobody knew what brought Vidal all the way down from the big city to a tiny town like Cedar Grove. Call it fate, call it destiny, call it tax evasion. Point is, it was Vidal that got this whole story started when she drove her rusty old Chevy Nova into the side of Ray Jean's diner. Call it fate, call it destiny, call it a woman fishing through her purse for a cigarette. Any way you look at it, it wasn't a very good foot to start off on, mind you, but it sure made for an exciting day of gossip in Cedar Grove. Luckily, Vidal was only a block away from the Cedar Grove Body Shop where she met the man who's the reason this whole story is. The charming prince.

Now don't go conjuring up images of this charming prince 'cause he wasn't exactly what you'd expect. He was a nice quiet man who never made a fuss with looks that I refer to as in t'middle. He wasn't exactly good looking and wasn't exactly bad looking, he was just, you know, in t'middle. He wasn't rich, and he wasn't poor, and unlike his three older brothers who had gone off to seek their fortunes and found 'em, this last boy never saw fit to leave Cedar Grove. He fixed fenders for a living and never really saw much reason to do more than that. He knew it wasn't gonna make him rich but it paid the bills and occasionally he had some left over for them fancy night crawlers over at *Buster's Bait and Tackle.* He fit into that town nice and easy as the steeple on top of the Cedar Grove Baptist Church. Something you saw every day but never really stopped and took notice of. Aside from his kinsfolk, most folks didn't know his real name. When folks talked about him they'd just say, "You know the one, he's that there Fender Fella."

But Vidal saw more than that when he handed her the quote to fix her car and she grabbed his palm and read it. She saw what other folks didn't. She saw a kind soul and a lingering sadness. Not the sorrowful kind of sadness that keeps you up at night or makes some folks turn to the drink, but the lonely kind of sorrow that never really goes away till you fall in love. Fender Fella would never admit it but Vidal knew – she hadn't won the Association's Crystal Palm Award for nothing.

She knew that Fender Fella missed his mamma who had passed away a couple years back. The only woman who could make Fender Fella laugh. And he hadn't laughed since. Vidal knew sure as anything that he needed a woman. Not a movie star kind of woman, or a Martha Stewart kind of woman, or a proponent of world peace kind of woman, or a therapist kind of woman. Not even a woman with good child-bearin' hips as was considered a fine asset in Cedar Grove. He needed a woman who would make him laugh. Plain and simple. A woman to stand by him when times were tough. A woman who could hold the other end of the fender when he was banging out a particularly nasty dent. And whether he liked it or not Vidal was gonna make it happen. Most women don't require approval when it comes to matters of the fixing up persuasion, especially Fairy Godmothers. After all, they are in the business of making dreams come true. Well, them and the lingerie industry.

So Vidal was on a mission and it didn't take long for her to find a princess. You could say they just ran into each other – literally. Call it fate, call it destiny, call it a woman reaching into the bottom of her purse for her hairspray. Vidal met her princess at the expense of another fender, but a princess just the same. Too bad she had to go through her mother to get there.

You see, Vidal ran her rusty old Chevy Nova into the side of none other than Porticia May Duberry, who jumped out of her car, mouth running like a plump turkey the day before Thanksgiving. Porticia was one of them types of women that give women a bad name. If you was to come up with a recipe for that woman it would go as follows:

> Three cups of irritation, a dash of aggravation
> One cup of sweetn'r, the artificial kind of course
> One teaspoon full of compassion for the homeless on Easter and Christmas
> A hint of spiteful
> A dash of hateful
> Three cups materialism, two cups greed
> One teaspoonful of sincerity followed close by a tablespoon of boastful pride

Put it all together and you had Porticia May DuBerry, obviously not one of her husband's favorite dishes 'cause the man did everything in his power to stay away. Some folks say it was his hard work that made Beauregard DuBerry the powerful man he was, owning a string of dairy farms spanning three states. Others say it was more like the power of a nagging woman on his heels. Ain't no better motivation to become a workaholic than that. Probably why he bought that second home in Cedar Grove. Another completely foreign concept to the folks in Cedar Grove since most of 'em had a hard enough time just paying for the one they got. Anyway, aside from her unwavering goal of being the most irritating and overbearing woman in Cedar Grove, Porticia May DuBerry's prime mission at the moment was to find a husband for her only daughter, known to most in town as the dairy princess.

It was common knowledge in Cedar Grove that once you reached a certain age you got married. And if you didn't, folks would set to whispering. The newlyweds would give you looks of pity, the younger women would desperately pray into their pillows at night that they'd never end up like you, and the menfolk would shake their heads and look at you like you'd done grown an extra head, wondering what horrible secret you was hiding that kept you from finding a fellow. And the oldest women in town would commence to plottin'. 'Cause there ain't nothing with more determination than a woman that's set her mind to fixin' somebody up. And the mamma is usually the worst one of the bunch, especially Porticia May DuBerry. And good thing she was so determined, with a daughter like Hortence. Thank goodness they had money 'cause that was just about the only thing they had that could marry that girl off.

Hortence, aka the dairy princess, wasn't considered beautiful by anybody's definition. She wasn't breathtaking and she wasn't hairy or nothing, she was just in t'middle. She wasn't talented, didn't care to be. She couldn't cook, didn't have to. She wasn't nice, didn't see the point. And she wasn't happy, didn't know how to be. In fact, she was a nasty spoiled little brat who was too accustomed to getting her own way and not accustomed enough to having a switch upside her rear end.

But she was the rich dairy princess and there were plenty of men who were interested. Hortence knew that she could afford to be choosy so she developed a list of "requirements," so to speak.

Mamma, dear Mamma, the princess would say
When you go looking for husbands today
Make sure he has muscles and abs made of steel
A rear end that breaks glass, and some raw man appeal.

Mamma dear Mamma, before I get hitched
Let's call up his banker and make sure he's rich
Not just a little, not just well off, you know
Mamma, please make sure he's rolling in dough.

His eyes must be blue and his eyelashes curly
His voice must be deep and his chest strong and burly,
A full head of hair, and please none on his back
And I'd prefer blond, as a matter of fact.

Mamma, dear Mamma, please listen up close,
My husband has got to be richer than most.
I'd prefer he not snore, I don't care if he's smart
And I ain't in this for love, so he don't need no heart.

Anyway, Vidal runs into these two colorful characters and the mamma's droning on and on about how she'll never get her daughter married off now that she's been wrecked and Hortence is running off at the mouth about more requirements she's come up with for her future husband, most of them of the financial nature, and both those mouths just yapping at full speed, heads bobbing up and down like they was two chickens singing a duet. Most folks would have sold their own brother to get out of that situation but Vidal was transpired, or is it transfigured, or transfixed? Shoot, she was mesmerized cause she was picking up them psychiatric vibrations like nothing she'd ever felt before. And she knew. She knew that the dairy princess, spoiled as she was, had some potential underneath that layer of brat. What she needed (aside from a swift kick in the rear) was a good man to straighten her out once and for all. Vidal had just found Fender Fella's dairy princess. And she was just what Fender Fella needed, too, though you can't really see it now but Vidal could 'cause she had this way of seeing straight through to the destiny of the situation. Too bad this view of hers didn't tell her how to make that happen. But it don't matter. Vidal was convinced and she commenced to planning a love connection.

Now every good fairy tale's got a fancy ball in it but Cedar Grove didn't know nothing about fancy balls. What they knew about was clogging. And take a fancy ball with horse drawn carriages and billowy dresses, throw it into Cedar Grove, and you got the Cedar Grove Annual Sweet Potato Dance at Skeeter's Barn with shiny patent leather clogging shoes, red checked gingham and petticoats and John Deeres and pickups with muddy tires lined up down the street. And this year word had got out that Porticia May DuBerry was gonna use this dance to find her daughter a husband once and for all. And that "word" coincidentally landed directly in Vidal's ear as is often the case in stories of the magical nature. But Vidal had one problem to work out. How in the world was she gonna make sure Fender Fella was at that dance?

Vidal spent some great thought on it. Why just the other day when he was banging out another dent in her fender he had told her that dances weren't his thing, just a bunch of nonsense in his opinion and he didn't have time in his life for nonsense. You see Fender Fella, bless his heart, was not exactly what you'd call on the cutting edge of the social set in Cedar Grove, as humble as that social set may have been. An exciting night to Fender Fella was when his television could pick up the Bass Fishing Tournament over in Garnett County and salisbury steak TV dinners were marked down half off. Just about the only thing that man cared about was fenders. Vidal's eyebrows shot up. She had a plan.

Fender Fella got the call after supper. The frantic call from Vidal, that palm readin' quack, as he referred to her, calling up in a panic 'cause she'd done busted up another fender in the parking lot of Skeeter's Barn and would he please hurry and come fix the other car before they caught wind of it, 'cause if one more person found out that her fender had done molested another fender, well surely she'd be kicked out of Cedar Grove or burned at the stake one. Fender Fella assured her that to his knowledge no one in Cedar Grove had ever been burned at a stake but that he would be right over. Vidal instructed him to come inside Skeeter's Barn and get her since it was dark out and not a good idea for a lady to be standing alone in a parking lot where she might be taken advantage of. Fender Fella left right away, trying to imagine the poor soul that would dare take advantage of Vidal.

Meanwhile, back at Skeeter's Barn, the available men and even some of the not so available men were tripping over themselves to get to the dairy princess because word was out that she was a'looking. Not a looker mind you, we've already covered that ground, but looking for the man who would take her as a bride and one day be the heir to the dairy throne. Just watching them men all trying to outdo the others was entertaining to say the least.

> Hortence, Hortence, may I have this dance?
> You look prettier than all the models in France.
> Hortence, dear Hortence, did you see my car?
> Gold package once owned by a movie star.
>
> Hortence, oh Hortence would you like some punch?
> Hear are some daisies, I picked you a bunch.
> Look at my suit, hand tailored and sewn.
> Just imagine the dresses that you would own.
>
> Hortence, dear Hortence, oh please marry me.
> My checking account will beat his times three.
> Hortence, dear Hortence, don't listen to him.
> My muscles are bigger than his at the gym.
>
> I'll write poems of love, I'll send flowers every day.
> I have six heads of cattle, three more on the way.
> I can play the guitar, I can take out my eye.
> Hortence, dear Hortence, please don't pass me by.

These men were pulling out all the stops to get that dairy princess's attention and it was really quite pathetic 'cause it was painfully obvious that it wasn't her looks, and it wasn't her talents, and it wasn't her personality, but her money that they was after. Hortence didn't seem to mind and was eating up all this attention like a chocolate hot fudge sundae. Vidal had been stuck to her side all night, doing everything in her power to find some reason for Hortence to turn down each man that approached and desperately wishing that Fender Fella would hurry up and get there.

Fender Fella arrived just as Hortence was being crowned Cedar Grove Sweet Potato Queen, much to the dismay of Irmadene Jean Jones who supposedly was a shoe-in for the prize since she was the prettiest girl in Cedar Grove. Folks were whispering that it was rigged, which it was. It had cost Mr. Beauregard DuBerry a pretty penny to convince those judges that Hortence deserved the crown.

Hortence didn't even notice Fender Fella enter Skeeter's Barn. Vidal motioned wildly for him to come join her, but Fender Fella just stood by the door and waited.

Vidal pointed him out to Hortence, who was not the least bit impressed because if there was one skill she did have it was being able to take one look at somebody and calculate their net worth. And it didn't take a rocket scientist to figure this one out. Muddy boots, worn jeans, leathery hands, dirt under the nails. All translated into one word. Poor. Next.

"But Hortence," said Vidal, not ready to give up 'cause after all, destiny was at stake. "Seem's like he's the only man in here not paying you any attention. Hhmmm. Fancy that." Hortence's head whipped around in a circle so fast she just about stared herself in the eyes, which just goes to prove that there ain't no bigger challenge to a woman than a man who ain't interested. And that, my friends, was the moment when them tables turned.

Hortence did everything in her power to get that man's attention, from batting her eyes, to flipping her hair, to walking past him so many times she started to get shin splints. She even lifted her skirt at one point like a shameless hussy. Still nothing. And the evening ended without so much as a how do you do.

And who could blame him's what I say. She was a spoiled rotten brat and everybody in town knew it. Dairy princess or dirt farmer, it was all the same to him. Just so happened that Fender Fella was one man who couldn't be bought.

Hortence went home in tears, so Hortence's mamma went home in tears. And Vidal stood there fuming in the parking lot while Fender Fella banged out the dents in her Nova that she'd gone to such great trouble to put there this afternoon. She was starting to question her gift and went home that night to reconsider some fallback options.

But Hortence didn't sleep because she was devising a plan of her own to win that man if it was the last thing she did. She stayed up all night but in her eyes it was worth it. And it would all happen at the parade the following day.

Every year the day after the Cedar Grove Sweet Potato Dance and crowning of the Cedar Grove Sweet Potato Queen, there's a parade, and everybody who ain't already in the parade comes to support the community. Fender Fella was there 'cause Buford, the mechanic in his auto shop, was gonna be driving a car in the parade. Vidal was there 'cause she was still considering options for her second career and was toying with the idea of being a parade planner. And Hortence DuBerry, Sweet Potato Queen, was there 'cause she had her very own float covered in streamers and flowers made out of tissue that the youngsters over at the Cedar Grove Baptist Church spent three nights making. And of course, sweet potatoes, hand sewn by Norma Ray Peterson every year ever since the last year they used real ones and learned that could have tragic consequences if landing in the wrong hands.

Hortence's float was behind the Cedar Grove fire truck, where Harvey Potts threw candy from the front widow, and in front of Cleetus Harley's flatbed of prize winning pigs rolling around in their slop, snorting happily at all the excitement. Following them was Old Man Peabody's prized stallion who'd never really won a race, well, never really even raced at all, but was from the very same bloodline of a horse that got replaced at the last minute in the Kentucky Derby twenty years ago.

Then you had the marching band from over at the high school in their costumes made by Norma Ray Peterson the year before she got her glasses. No one had the heart to tell her that marching band uniforms needed neckholes like anything else and everybody ended up having to cut their own at the last minute. And so on and so on down the parade line was a collection of local business folks showing off their wares.

Since Hortence didn't really have any talent to speak of, never really seeing the point in cultivating anything of any particular value, and since obviously Fender Fella was not enamoured by her womanly ways as much as she threw 'em in his face, she had only one choice, that one thing that always lays waiting for those girls in Cedar Grove who come up short – baton twirling. Didn't matter that she'd never even seen one up close, she was desperate. She even found one of them batons up in her mamma's attic that you could light on the ends and she stayed up all night long practicing her little fanny off.

Timing was definitely on her side that day as Hortence's float neared Fender Fella who was standing in front of Vidal whose psychic vibes told her, *something's going on here,* and she gave Hortence a thumbs up.

When Hortence was sure that she was in the direct line of her charming prince she took a deep breath, lit her baton, and started to twirl. She twirled like she'd never twirled before. She twirled as if her life depended on it. But it wasn't exactly Fender Fella's eye that she caught, but the eyes of Old Man Peterson's prize stallion. And it wasn't exactly awe in his eyes but cold-blooded fear and if you've ever been around a horse that's afraid , well it ain't pretty. And that horse let out a blood-curdling teeth-baring neigh and stood directly up on his back legs and then ran like he'd never run before. Only he wasn't exactly the smartest horse in the world and instead of running away from the origin of his fear, he ran towards it. Ran right into the Cedar Grove Sweet Potato Float, knocking Miss Hortence right off her feet where amazingly enough she lands directly on that horse's back still holding her baton, much to the delight of the crowd but to the dismay of that horse who now realized that the fire was on his back. And he let out another terrified squeal and reared up again, this time throwing Hortence DuBerry off his back with such force that she went flying backwards and landed — oh — it's almost too painful for words — directly into Cleetus's pig bed with a splat that sent mud flying clear over to the next county and the parade came to a screeching halt.

Hortence came up to her knees still holding that baton, covered in slimy pig slop, looked like something my dog threw up once underneath a living room chair. It wasn't pretty. And she started to wail while everyone stared for there wasn't anyone (not even her own mamma) who was willing to climb in that pig bed after her. Or I should say almost no one. 'Cause there was one person in that crowd that felt a tug. A tug on his heart that he couldn't explain.

Fender Fella stared at Hortence DuBerry and the left corner of his mouth turned up, and then the right, and then his face broke out into a smile so big and bright that it transformed his whole face. And he started to laugh. A deep laugh bursting up through the bottom of his gut. A laugh that had been buried for a long, long time. And there wasn't really any thinking to what he did next. He just did it. I guess that's the way it is with destiny and fairy tales.

Fender Fella pushed his way through the crowd till he got to the pig pen. He held onto the side and hoisted his body right over like he did it every day. The crowd gasped in amazement. Why this was more exciting than that TV movie of the week where the mamma falls in love with her nanny's kid. This was better than gossip. This was gossip at its birth.

Hortence stopped crying and stared at Fender Fella, not knowing what to make of him trudging through that pig slop towards her, but it was a humbling experience for that dairy princess, who was sure that all chances to get that charming prince had passed her by. And then (oh my, this part always tears me up) then, in front of God and everybody, Fender Fella picks up the dairy princess like she was light as a rag doll and kissed her. It was beautiful. And not one of them chicken peck kind of kisses either, but the kind of kiss that sends electricity shooting straight down to yer toes.

And like most fairy tales it happened in that one single moment. That one single moment where fate steps in and makes all your dreams come true and fills up all your empty places. And they've been together ever since.

Oh, she still has her moments. It ain't always easy to up and leave behind the person you was. Especially with that spoiled streak she's got. And he still refuses to do nothing more than fix fenders for a living despite her attempts to turn him into an investment banker. But they're good for each other. And they've lived, for the most part, happily ever after.

And in case you're wondering what ever happened to Miss Vidal, well, she claims she stuck around Cedar Grove 'cause Fender Fella needed someone with her poor driving skills to keep his business afloat. But in truth — well, let's just say that the day of that parade there was more than one princess meeting her charming prince.

The Devil and Blackjack Cratchett

Gather round me close
Lend your ear and sit a spell
On this spooky Halloween
Where the ghosts and goblins dwell,

Watch out for moving shadows
Watch out for howling wind
It's Halloween, a scary scene,
The ghosts have come again.

It's the night where spirits moan
Where evil overshadows light,
Things that creak and things that squeak
And things that go bump in the night.

So lean in a little closer.
Breathe in and then exhale.
Relax and rest a while
As I spin my spooky tale.

For if you listen long enough
To your storytelling host,
You will hear the story
Of Black Jack Cratchett's ghost.

****

Have you ever seen a ghost?
Do you know one personally by name?
Have you heard howling winds that moan
And branches scrape your window pane?
Have you ever felt a chill
Creep slowly up your spine.
Because you heard the slightest noise.
A creak or moan or whine?

Have you peeked from beneath your covers,
Looked for shadows by your closet door,
Made sure your feet didn't dangle over
What may be lurking down on the floor?

Have you stared into the dark
With eyes open wide in fright?
Have you ever heard a far off wolf
Howling in the night?

Well everything you see and hear
Has a common explanation.
It's not the boogie man or a ghost,
Just your imagination.

There are no such things as ghosts.
Those things are only in your head.
There are no one-eyed monsters
Lurking underneath your bed.

My mamma says it's make believe,
That ghosts do not exist.
They aren't all floating eerily
In a graveyard's foggy mist.

Mamma says there are no witches
With warty nose and bubbling pot,
And my mamma's always right.
Or then again, maybe not.

One thing that's so much fun about Halloween is that you get to talk about scary stuff. And I don't mean scary as in what my mamma looked like first thing in the morning with her cold cream pack and pink sponge curlers in her hair. I'm not talking about scary as in the time Cleetus Harley 'bout got himself runned over by that milk truck, on account of he had up and fallen asleep right in the smack dab middle of the road after the Cedar Grove Winterfest, when someone had the bright idea to serve something called a Mint Julep which most folk in town thought was some fancy kind of punch.

I'm talking 'bout scarified things like ghosts and witches and devils and demons and premonitions and superstitions and apparitions and crooked politicians, and drowning while fishing, and sorry magicians, and things that go bump in the night. For a small town like Cedar Grove with its two stoplights total, they had more than their share of scary stuff. Like that peculiar sound the wind made whenever it moved a certain way through the trees. Sounded like something moaning far off in the distance.

There was this one Halloween that the younguns all heard tell of a ghost story about the devil waiting in the trees to steal a youngun's soul and so from that day on that spooky noise turned into a song: *Soul, soul, soul to keep. Devil's waiting in your sleep.* Yeah, folks in Cedar Grove weren't too terribly scared of ghosts, not sure they even believed in 'em. But if you even mentioned the devil you'd see blood draining out of more than one face.

Whenever the kids would hear that moaning sound in the trees they'd think of that song and there wasn't a kid in Cedar Grove with a foot hanging over the edge of the bed at night. Some of 'em even took the utmost of safety precautions by burying themselves up underneath their bedcovers, completely hidden 'cept for that one hole they'd created for their nose to poke out of so they could breathe. 'Cause everybody knows if you can't see the demon then it can't see you.

I guess all towns have scary stories like the time every last light in Cedar Grove went out. Every light from front porches to ovens to cash registers to digital watches to car dashboards to the younguns' tennis shoes. Might not seem like such a big deal to you but it was to the folks in Cedar Grove on account of it was at the exact moment that Stella crooked her head, twitched her eye, and cast a wicked spell over the entire town.

Stella was a gypsy woman traveling through Cedar Grove on foot one crisp fall day. She dropped into Ray Jean's diner asking for a cup of hot tea, which cast suspicion from the get-go cause everybody knows the only way to drink tea is cold and sweet. Stella Lunella was her name and like I said she was a gypsy. And while most folks in town weren't really sure what a gypsy was, they were convinced it couldn't be good. What with a name like Stella Lunella she surely wasn't from around them parts and that was enough to cast doubt from the start.

When Nana Hawkins shuffled up to Stella Lunella and asked her business there, Stella said she was traveling through town on her quest for the spirit of the truth, which sent the pastor over at the Cedar Grove Baptist Church into a frenzied state of prayer and near about caused a chain reaction of heart attacks through the sewing circle of Cedar Grove. They hadn't had anything this interesting to talk about during their quilting bee since the time Skeeter Jones got himself arrested for making his own moonshine and carted over to Garnett County in one of them official prisoner trucks while his poor hound dog chased behind him till his poor little legs give out.

One look at Stella Lunella and her gold spun skirt and earrings shaped like the moon and they were convinced she had her a direct dedicated line to the devil. And women started guarding their men, since everybody knows that wicked women who drink hot tea can't be trusted. And her eyes, the way they bulged out like a bullfrog's and were lined with thick blackness and the lids were covered in a mint green color like pistachio ice cream, and the way they would just set on you and kind of quiver. Well, it was just downright freaky and folks wouldn't look her in the eye for fear that she'd cast some wicked spell and their body parts would start falling off.

> Her name was Stella,
> Stella Lunella,
> A gypsy who's out to steal your fella
> *Ooooooooooo*
> Stella
> Stella Lunella ....
> Magic and passion
> Were always her fashion
> Oh Lunella
> She was no good... Stella Lunella

Anyway, cast a spell is precisely what Stella did. And anybody who's ever heard one single fairy tale in their entire lives would know that when somebody casts a spell it is to be taken with the utmost of seriousness.

Folks claim it was all John Henry Junior's fault that she cast that spell, on account of he was a troublemaker and always looking for an opportunity to make a dollar, especially at somebody else's expense. Before Stella Lunella's hot tea was even cold, John Henry Junior had started yet another one of his business endeavors and had the kid folk of Cedar Grove lined up around the block with quarter in hand (or something of similar value) to see Stella Lunella, a real live gypsy of the highest order and better all come take a look now so's she'll appreciate your interest and won't cast a spell on you, like making every meal you eat for the rest of your days taste like mushy Brussels sprouts.

John Henry started telling the kid folk that Stella would even cast their very own spell if'n they brought a whole dollar. All you had to do was bring your spell written out on a piece of paper: For example, "Please Mrs. Gypsy woman, make Franklin Peterson throw up again in math class this Wednesday so we won't have to take that test." "Please your Gypsy Majesty, turn my rusty old bike into one of them scooters I saw on the back of the Frosted Fritters Box." John Henry had an imagination that wouldn't quit but he had no idea he was playing with trouble, 'cause everybody knows that nothing good can come out of taking a walk on the dark side.

He must have made her mad, 'cause next thing you know Stella was cocking her head and quivering her eyes, and she raised her arms up in the air, shook 'em wildly back and forth in a shivering motion that traveled through her whole body like a seizure. And then she made this gesture with her hand that just screamed out *Curse on all of ya'll* and she left Ray Jean's Diner with a dramatic sweeping of her arms, as if to say her work there was done, leaving what folks swore was a cloud of dust behind her and a cheap tip on the counter, which just proved their point that Stella was no good. And it was at that moment that every light in town went out. And there was pandemonium.

Folks were wailing and crying and testifying, sobbing and robbing and glorifying, cursing and crooning and deep heavy sighing, all of 'em thinking "I'm dyin', I'm dyin'." All of 'em wailing together in unison like some country choir gone out of tune. And then the lights came back on and everybody was still there and every body part accounted for, all except for Chigger who was missin' an arm, but that was missin' before the lights went out so it was okay. Stella was gone. They never saw her again.

Anyway, folks blamed John Henry for getting Stella all fired up, but truth be told there was a lot of craziness going on at the time, what with the full moon and all. Sometimes rumors can get started by the wrong people, like crazy Katie who just the day before had been found sitting directly in the middle of that fountain outside of *Buster's Bait and Tackle* serving tea and crumpets to George Washington. Can't say I've ever had me a crumpet, have you? And by the way, she was drinking her tea cold and sweet.

But there's many a folk who are convinced that it was that horrible spell (folks liked to exaggerate, I mean if you're gonna tell somebody you been struck with a spell, you might as well say it was a horrible spell). Anyway, they figured it was that spell that triggered that string of violent thunderstorms that triggered Widow Willowby's rheumatism that triggered another one of Grandma Nelly's premonitions that triggered the Cratchetts moving to town, that triggered the murder of Black Jack Cratchett, one of the meanest men to ever reside in Cedar Grove. Only one meaner than Black Jack Cratchett was Black Jack Cratchett's ghost. That is, if you're the sort to believe in ghosts. And I ain't saying I am, I'm just telling the story as I heard it. But I'm getting ahead of myself. So I'll back up to Grandma Nelly and her premonition.

Grandma Nelly was the oldest woman in Cedar Grove and some folks said they'd never seen her when she wasn't old. Grandma Nelly could see things before they happened. Scenes played out in her head like a movie. When she walked down the street, with her silver hair flowing behind her, tree limbs rustled and dogs barked for no reason. She had an aura about her as some folks called it. Others said she was crazy and wasn't no such thing as seeing things before they happened. Some said she was clairvoyant and others said she was so wrapped up in the grips of the devil she'd like to never find her way out. But crazy or not, couldn't nobody dispute the fact that every premonition Grandma Nelly ever had came true.

She knew Cam Peterson was gonna have his gall bladder taken out three years before it happened. She knew the fate of Old Horace's hound dog that run out in front of that Speedy Express Van. She knew when times were hard and when folks were gonna lose their farms. It was a shame she wasn't a bettin' woman.

> Nelly, Nelly, Crazy Nelly,
> Sees things that ain't happened yet.
>
> Nelly, Nelly, Crazy Nelly,
> Knows the fate of your family pet.
>
> Nelly, Nelly, Crazy Nelly,
> Better not show up in her dream,
>
> Nelly, Nelly, Crazy Nelly,
> 'Cause you know what that might mean.
>
> Nelly, Nelly, Crazy Nelly,
> If she ever dreams of you,
>
> Nelly, Nelly, Crazy Nelly
> It might just mean the end of you.

But the premonition that folks remember most, the premonition that will still make the hair stand straight up on the arm of anyone who remembers it, the premonition that folks don't like to talk about in a voice bigger than a whisper was when she saw the murder of Black Jack Cratchett before Black Jack Cratchett even moved into town.

It was in the middle of the night and it was a cold windy night and the tree limbs were scratching against the window pane and a cold chill moved through Grandma Nelly's bedroom, which was always the way her premonitions started out. And plain as day Nelly saw a man with a sharp face and a wicked eye take a bullet straight through the heart. It was raining, of course.

One of them nights where the wind is singing its song. *Soul, soul, soul to keep. Devil's waiting in your sleep.* Yeah, Grandma Nelly saw the murder and she saw who did it too.

They moved into that big old house at the bottom of Third Street sitting cattycorner to *Harvey's Ice Cream Stand / Hotdog Stand / Sunglass Hut.* The Cratchetts, that is. This was before the house was turned into *Beauregard's Funeral Home for the Dearly Departed Pets of Cedar Grove,* which by the way isn't a very profitable venture. It was later turned into *Myrlene, Vyrlene, and Shirlene's House of Beauty.* Back then, the house was boarded up and empty and rumored to be haunted. And there wasn't one person in town who knew the Cratchetts or any of their kin. So folks was naturally suspicious.

Folks in Cedar Grove did not take well to strangers 'cause strangers meant change, and change was not a good thing. So most folks didn't care for the new family that moved into the house at the bottom of Third Street one bit. Especially when they found out that family didn't have any children, a completely unheard of concept in Cedar Grove, where younguns multiplied like kudzu.

The Cratchetts' first night in the house, nobody had saw 'em or heard 'em despite peering through the blinds, making up excuses to drive past, and sending their kids to go spying through the windows, cause if they were caught wouldn't nobody be accused of spying what with them bein' children and all. But nobody caught even the tiniest whisper of a glimpse of a person anywhere around the place. Had it not been for the boards removed and curtains put up and drawn closed they would have sworn the house was still empty.

Over time, folks did catch glimpses of Jack Cratchett and his wife Norma. Menfolk saw Jack most 'cause he would come down the way whenever there was a card game starting up. Jack was a gambler, a serious gambler, the kind of gambler that would drive over to Garnett County if that was the only place he could play him some Black Jack. That's how he got the nickname Black Jack Cratchett. Black Jack Cratchett had a wife named Norma — a quiet mousy little thing that wouldn't never look you straight in the eye. Black Jack Cratchett was so mean and controlling to that woman that she might as well have been wearing a leash. He didn't let her out much.

Gambling was not looked upon kindly by folks in Cedar Grove, or at least by the ones not doing the gambling. Like Nana Hawkins who was known to speak her mind whenever and however to whomever she saw fit on account of she considered herself to be that age of womanhood where you can do no wrong. Nana Hawkins made it quite clear that money come by the dishonest way is devil's money plain and simple and if you questioned her she'd just cut her eyes and accuse you of disrespectin' your elders. She was a piece of work, that Nana Hawkins, but if you knew the end of the Black Jack tale like I do, well, you might think that for once Nana Hawkins had a point. I'll let you decide.

Anyway, Black Jack gambled. He drank corn liquor straight out of the bottle, smoked fancy cigars, cursed from here to Wednesday, and most folks were convinced that he had already earned him one of them permanent seats in the devil's house right alongside May Belle Meriweather, that painted up hussy who once had the nerve of opening up one of her businesses in Cedar Grove (and I use that word rather loosely).

Aside from being what folks considered the most consistent sinner you'd ever run across, Black Jack Cratchett on his very best day was a miserable nasty wretch of a man with a sharp tongue and a sharp heart to match. Black Jack treated his hound dog better than his wife Norma, who folks claimed was a saint for the simple reason that she stayed married to that man without killing him in his sleep. There was only one thing that Black Jack loved — *m-o-n-e-y* — money. And rumor was he had lots of it.

Oh, he loved money. Loved the sounds of the coins rubbing together, the smell of a fresh dollar bill, the feel of it between his fingers. Some claimed the man rolled around in it when wasn't nobody looking. All that money and he never spent a dime 'cept on fancy cigars and corn liquor. The rest he hid. Didn't trust another living soul with it, not the bank, not even his own wife. Wouldn't tell her where it was hid, and even worse, made the poor thing work her fingers to the nubs cleaning houses. He didn't care. All he cared about was his money and because it consumed his every waking moment, he kept moving it from hiding place to hiding place. But that money was tainted, or so Nana Hawkins said. Every penny.

> Black Jack Cratchett was a nasty man
> Ruled his wife with an iron hand
> Never laughed and he never smiled
> And when he drank he turned mean and wild.
>
> Black Jack Cratchett was a gambling man
> Just how bad you'd never understand
> He was loud and rude and a troublemaker
> Once bet his own wife but nobody'd take her.
>
> Black Jack Cratchett was rotten to his core
> Had money in piles and yet he wanted more
> And his evilness grew so big, I'm told,
> That Black Jack Cratchett finally bet his own soul.
>
> Now Norma Cratchett was the quiet sort
> Not one to make a fuss or give a nasty retort
> She was kind and giving with a heart so big
> So why in the world did she marry that pig?
>
> Norma Cratchett, folks couldn't understand
> Why she didn't take a skillet to that nasty man.
> How some people tick, we'll never know
> Why that should be a feature on the Oprah show.

They say that selling your soul is not a very wise thing to do and that's why evil came knockin' on Black Jack's door and struck him with this horrible illness out of the blue one winter. An illness that made horrible pus-like things grow all over his body. An illness with a name so long you couldn't even pronounce it, much less spell it. An illness that the doctors couldn't trace back to anything and had no cure in sight. An illness that took away Black Jack's memory. Some folks called it the fever and others said it was that gypsy's curse. Others called it amnesia, but most just called it the devil taking his due. For the one thing

Black Jack loved the most was money and he had bushels of it. Just couldn't remember where he hid it. Now if that ain't justice. Anyway, if you thought Black Jack was a nasty man before, he was even nastier now.

So nasty they said he started taking it out on his wife in ways that a husband don't need to be doing. And he was consumed with finding his money even more than he was before, if you can believe it. Spent every waking moment deep into the night searching until that dreadful night when he didn't have to search no more. *Soul, soul, soul to keep. Devil's waiting in your sleep.*

It happened during that storm that caused the flood that wiped out Old Man Byerly's place. Folks were so busy pitching in to help that nobody was paying attention to the Cratchett house and the storm was raging with such fierceness that nobody heard the shot. Folks later found out that Sheriff Henry got a call — a quiet voice on the other end saying her husband had been shot dead. And by the time word got round to the rest of the folk who were still busy over at the Byerly place, what was left of it, all they were told was that Black Jack Cratchett was dead and Norma was gone to live with her sister in some city out west. No charges were made against anybody and the case was dropped that very day.

Folks still aren't sure just what happened that night – the night Black Jack Cratchett took a bullet to the heart. There are different rumors depending on who you ask. Some say it was an angry man who'd been cheated in a poker game. Others say it was a robber trying to get a hold of his money. But I doubt you'll find one person who felt sorry for the man who hoarded his money and died without another living soul knowing where it was hid. Folks looked all over for months till they finally figured maybe he didn't have all that money after all. Maybe the fellow who shot him took off with it. And folks finally gave up, figuring it was tainted money to begin with and probably better left alone. But that ain't the end of the story, no sir. And if I didn't hear it from so many people I wouldn't believe it. But you just can't help but wonder.

Black Jack was dead. Let there be no doubt about that. There was a body and a funeral, or at least they tried to have a funeral but wouldn't nobody come 'cept a few folks who were thinking there might be some free food. And when they found nothing to eat they left without so much as a good riddance. And John Henry Junior and some of the other younguns came by on account of it's just not every day you get to see a real live dead body. Anyway, Black Jack was as dead as dead gets. But sometimes – at least according to folks who believe in such things – well, sometimes they don't stay dead. They come back, only they don't come back all the way so most of the time you can't see 'em. You can only hear 'em, or smell 'em, or feel 'em brush by your body like a breath of wind. At least that's what I've heard.

You see the thing of it is, Black Jack ain't gone. He's still roaming through the streets and houses of Cedar Grove looking for his money. You think I'm lying but Old Man Peterson hears drawers slamming in his sleep every Thursday. Miss Bitsy keeps finding her kitchen cabinets opened come morning time. Lester Jenkins will swear on his very own mamma's grave that he can smell cigar smoke while he's brushing his teeth late at night. Sometimes on a beginning-of-the-summer kind of night when folks open their windows to hear the crickets while they sleep, there's some who live up close to the old Cratchett house who will swear that they hear muffled cursing outside their window. And there's been more than one person out to fetch the morning paper and found holes dug up fresh as the morning dew. Or stones overturned. I'm telling you he's looking for it. And they know by the hair standing up on their arms that Black Jack was there that night looking for his treasure. And sometimes late on a stormy night if you listen really close from underneath your bed covers you can almost hear the devil laughing over the howl of the wind.

Grandma Nelly never told anybody what she saw in that premonition and so folks have come to their own conclusions. What do I think? Well, Grandma Nelly became a very religious person after that. And you can come to any conclusion you want to from that but I'm gonna side with Nana Hawkins in that money come by the dishonest way is devil's money. And if you got any questions about that you just ask Black Jack Cratchett's ghost. He'll tell you what can happen when you sell your soul.

Mamma and the Prom

My mamma ran on one speed and that was high. She sandblasted her way through life with eyes closed, changing course sporadically and wondering at every turn should she have gone in the other direction. One arm cleaning, another arm baking, an ear to the phone, an eye out the window, and looking for miracles every step of the way. 'Cause my mamma believed in angels, ghosts, premonitions, superstitions, apparitions, and that anything dangling outside the ordinary was undoubtedly a sign from God. Some folks called her passionate. I called her a leech on my soul determined to hang there till she'd drained the very last drop of my existence. Okay, so I was a dramatic teenager, but my mamma did nothing in moderation.

Take Halloween, for instance. Used to be my favorite holiday as a kid until the year my mamma decided it would be cute if we wore matching costumes. Suddenly Wonder Woman isn't so cool anymore when you got your mamma close on your heels wearing the very same outfit. Only she thought fishnet hose would be a nice added touch. And she never could find one of them bodysuits that fit her robust frame so there was always a body part or two sticking out at the most inappropriate of times. Daddy used to walk behind her and say, "Woman, where'd you get them two pigs fightin' under a blanket?" Whatever he meant by that.

My mamma was not the sort of woman who simply lived life. She sucked every moment out of it like a thick chocolate shake running through a straw. She didn't walk if she could dance. She didn't talk if she could sing. She didn't cry, she bellowed. She didn't hug, she crushed. She didn't watch her life, she performed it. I probably would have admired her. If she'd been somebody else's mamma. No, I'd been caught up one too many times in her spotlight.

My first bra, for example. Mamma had it bronzed. Still sitting up on that mantelpiece beside my brother's silver-plated retainer. When I was in grade school, I was in the spelling bee and Mamma made me a dress. Yellow with black rings. Get it? Spelling bee. Yeah, she thought it was clever too. And then she decided to make the rest of the family outfits to match and, whenever somebody would comment on it, Mamma would buzz loudly and pretend to sting 'em. I didn't think you could be a social outcast in the second grade. I was wrong.

When it come time to tell me about the birds and the bees, Mamma didn't do it like the other mammas. She didn't give me a book or a video. She didn't explain it in a way that didn't really answer any questions but was relatively painless to all parties involved. Not my mamma. She explained it in full vivid detail.

Being the modern woman that she considered herself to be, she decided to give me real life examples from her own journey to womanhood. Every gruesome detail. That woman painted a picture for me I still can't get out of my head to this day. I never was able to look my daddy in the eye again. Then Mamma continued her training session with a dramatic interpretation of a woman's guide to self-piety and preservation, complete with excerpts from magazines and afternoon talk shows on the subject of men's lust and rejection. Followed by forty-seven scripture references to God's thinking on the subject which she lovingly had typed up on strips of paper and laminated so I could carry 'em around with me in my purse.

Then she told me that if I ever was to find myself in the "family way" she'd be there for me. But that Daddy would hunt me down, chop me up like barbecue, and serve me on toast. Before I had time to recover from the whole horrible ordeal, mamma had the audacity to serve corndogs for dinner. It is no wonder I need therapy.

My mamma was also one of those mothers who felt that childbirth had given her certain parental rights along with an open ticket to situations to which she otherwise wouldn't be invited. Mamma didn't question her right to be anywhere that involved one of her children. In Mamma's eyes, her children were simply extensions of herself. How could we experience life to its fullest without her being right there beside us to cheer us on?

That was cute for birthday parties and school plays. It was grudgingly acceptable for training bra dressing rooms and perm appointments. But somewhere between my first date and my honeymoon, it became unbearable. I have mellowed over time and have learned to forgive Mamma for her unwanted appearances over the years but there's just one thing I can't bring myself to forgive her for. Mamma showing up at my senior prom. Not only can I not forgive, I can't forget. Sometimes late at night I'll shoot up in my bed with a scream that sends my dog flying across the room, my body drenched in sweat and my heart racing. No, I wasn't dreaming of being chopped up to bits by a serial killer. I was dreaming of that moment when my date said the four words no girl ever wants to hear on prom night: "Is that your mother?"

Yes, my friends, it was my mother. The woman from whose loins I'd sprung, waving enthusiastically from the doors to our gym which had been transformed into a night under the stars. A night that smelled like sweat socks and basketballs, but a night under the stars all the same. Dad just stood there with this apologetic look on his face and a "what could I do" shrug of his shoulders. In case you've never been in that particular situation, it is hard to describe the thoughts that race through your mind as you review your options ranging from facing your fears to suicide. I took the high road and ran for the restroom like an overweight turkey the day before Thanksgiving. I hid there for a while trying to erase the mental image of my mamma wearing a mint green dress that matched mine only so many sizes bigger that she resembled some sort of tropical fruit. But girls kept coming into the restroom so much and talking about the loud old woman doing the limbo and singing with the band that I couldn't stand it any longer. I stood behind a plastic tree watching my date hit on a cheerleader and my mamma doing the electric slide and hitching her dress up to reveal, Lord help me, white fishnet hose – typical example of Mamma's fashion sense.

I gasped in horror when I saw Mamma downing a glass of punch. Mamma didn't know what seniors did to the punch on prom night. Mamma wasn't a drinker. Until that night. My mamma is an energetic person anyway. After a couple of glasses of that punch, she became the Road Runner on speed. I didn't know Mamma's body could do those things. I'm not sure she did either. I wanted to go find her and make her leave but every time she'd catch sight of me and yell, "Yoo hoo, honey," I just couldn't do it and I'd run to find another hiding spot.

As if things couldn't get any worse, Mamma became the hit of the prom. Someone even wrote her name in on the voting ballot for prom queen and, for the first time in the history of Cedar Grove High, humor won out over popularity. And much to Emma Hayes's dismay (most likely to break hearts her entire life), Mamma was voted prom queen and gave a tearful speech about having dreamed of this moment, followed by an off-key solo of *Wind Beneath My Wings* that had kids doubled over in laughter. Mamma didn't even notice. She was in the spotlight.

Mamma closed the place down that night. My date left with the cheerleader and I got a ride home with the gym coach, who lived on my street. My mamma got home later than I did, which just poured salt into the wound. She came barreling into my room to ask where I'd gotten off to and to relive every moment up to the point where she threw up in the parking lot. And how did I like her surprise?

I just looked at her. She had no idea what she had done to my life. I don't think she knows to this very day.

We have what we call the wall of fame running down the main hall of Cedar Grove High. It's decorated with pictures of great students and teachers throughout history, infamous football games and scholarships awarded. And right smack in the middle of it all, larger than life, is a framed photo of my mamma being crowned prom queen. At the time I thought that episode was the end of any claim I would ever have to a normal life. I had reached the bottom. But turns out it was only the beginning.

Heroes

John Henry saw the contest on the back of the Frosted Fritters box one morning in early fall. *Heroes From Around the World,* it said, but John Henry wasn't paying attention to that. He was paying attention to the prize. The coolest ten-speed chrome-plated dual-action silver-spiked deluxe-edition Sir Speed Racer bike ever to grace his presence. In that one second John Henry knew what it was like to want something so bad you would consider bargaining your very own soul for it. And all you had to do was write a paper. Submit a hero. One hundred words or less. The hero must have been born in your home town. Judging will be based on the hero's contribution to society. Employees of Frosted Fritters are not eligible.

John Henry's mind raced. He could write a paper. Why he'd even type it up. Wouldn't that impress them judges? Those judges, he corrected himself. He'd better start working on his grammar right now if he ever expected to win that bike. The bike. John Henry whispered the word with reverence. And he was only one hero away from getting it. The deadline was in three weeks. Three weeks to find a hero. Three weeks until all his dreams come true. He could do that with time left over. So John Henry Junior set out to find him a hero and what better place to start than in your very own house.

"Mamma," asked John Henry. "We got any heroes in our family? They've got to come from Cedar Grove."

"Don't think so, dear," said Mamma. "Go ask your father." So John Henry asked his daddy the same question.

"Born here in Cedar Grove?" his daddy asked. "No, not that I'm aware of. We come from a long line of fairly uneventful people, son. 'Cept for your cousin Nate that run that illegal moonshine operation up over the hill and 'bout got shot for it. Now you need stories about folks dancing on the wrong side of the law and we'll talk. But heroes? Try Widow Jenkins. She might know somebody."

"Why, sure," said Widow Jenkins. "There was Baker Simms who got a purple heart. And there was Minerva Potts who saved that little girl from drowning. And my uncle Herschel once ran into a burning building after a ferret. Does that count?

He didn't die or nothing but burned his eyebrows clear off his head. He looked like a freak show after that. He probably won't mind you writing about him. Oh wait, they've got to be born in Cedar Grove? No, none of 'em were born here. Sorry kiddo, try the Pastor. Maybe he knows somebody."

Pastor Isaiah wasn't any help either and just kept going on and on about heroes from the Bible, which didn't do John Henry much good since all those heroes back then never even heard of Cedar Grove much less come from there. Too bad Jesus wasn't from Cedar Grove. Couldn't beat that hero. Pastor suggested John Henry try Ned and Horace who were sitting out on their bench in front of the five and dime as usual.

"Hero?" asked Ned. "What'cha need a hero for?" John Henry explained the contest for as much good as it did considering Ned dozed off a couple of times in the process.

"I'm eighty-nine," said Horace. "I think anyone living to eighty-nine deserves to be called a hero."

"That ain't a hero, Horace," said Ned. "Heroes risk their lives for others. You ever risked your life for someone else?" Horace thought a minute.

"Can't say as I have. Once gave blood though. Ya think that counts?"

"Shoot no, Horace," said Ned. "That was probably tainted blood anyway. Wasn't that during your partyin' days?"

"Yeah, that was 'fore I turned Baptist and was warshed clean," said Horace. "Had some good times, though, before then. Remember that time we got caught smoking behind the outhouse and old Maybelle was doing her business and thought the outhouse was on fire." They snorted in laughter.

"Yeah," said Ned. "And she come running out of that outhouse with her pants around her knees screaming 'fire' and waving her hands in the air like she was surrendering to the Yankees. That sure was funny."

"Yeah, we laughed for days on that one."

"Too bad it was old Maybelle, made the story kind of frightening. Wish it had been Beatrice Peabody. Now she was a looker."

"Yeah," said Horace. And they sat staring off into the distance, lost in their boyhood fantasies.

"You need a hero, son, you ought to try over at Sunnyside Hills," said Ned. "Nursing homes is always a good place to look for heroes and they've got plenty of time to sit and chat too. But stay away from Myrtle Jones. She'll try to kiss on ya one minute, and the next she'll be beating you with her purse, thinking you're trying to steal it. And give my best to Ronny Sparks for me and tell him I'll be by next week to show him my new fishin' rod. You up for some fishin', Horace?" Horace nodded. John Henry took off down the street while Ned and Horace talked about fishing for a good thirty minutes and decided to take a nap instead.

John Henry and the other younguns in Cedar Grove had their own name for Sunnyside Hills. They called it the Wax Museum 'cause the people in there looked they were made of wax since they never moved or nothing and some of their faces were frozen in various expressions ranging from pain to discontent. Most of them stayed that way too even if you got up close and made funny faces at 'em which John Henry knew from experience. Some of 'em watched TV's that weren't even turned on. Francie Bell liked to watch *Jeopardy* over and over and kept yelling out that she wanted to buy a vowel even when you'd tell her that was the wrong game. So that's how come they called it the Wax Museum. Wasn't very polite but then sometimes kids aren't very polite. So John Henry figured a wax hero was better than no hero and he got there during Bingo so he had lots of choices 'cause they all come out for Bingo.

John Henry went up to one after the other asking were they a hero. Three hours later he'd met a professional diver, three teachers, a lady who almost made it to the Olympics for pole vaultin', and a man who thought he remembered being President, but no hero. John Henry was worn out but he kept picturing that new bike and his energy would be renewed. He was gonna try one more – that man over by the window wearing flannel pajamas and smoking a cigarette.

"Sir?" asked John Henry. "Are you by chance a hero?"

"A hero?" he asked quietly staring at John Henry like he was trying to place the family. "You one of the Henry kids?" John Henry nodded. "Good people, your family," he said. "Looking for a hero, eh? What kind of hero?"

"Any kind of hero, Sir. Like maybe you saved somebody from a fire, or disarmed a bomb, or maybe jumped out of a crashing train holding a little kid. Stuff like that." The man chuckled quietly. He had gentle eyes kind of like what John Henry imagined Santa's would be like. "Like a war hero maybe?" he asked. John Henry's eyes widened hoping beyond hope that this man's memory wasn't warped like some of the others.

"Yes, Sir!" said John Henry imagining that bike being delivered to his front door. "Are you a war hero?"

"Well, I'm not sure you'd call me a hero. I was a Colonel, served in World War II, Korea, and Vietnam. That's where I got the nickname Lucky Strike." John Henry's jaw dropped. A Colonel. A real live Colonel. He'd never seen one up close before. "How'd you get the nickname, Sir?" asked John Henry.

"Had three choppers shot out from under me in one day," he answered. "Survived all three crashes. Others didn't survive. But I lived through three helicopter crashes in one day. Started callin' me Lucky Strike. The fellas would touch me for good luck before going up on a mission. Lucky Strike. Gonna have that put on my tombstone if I have any say in it." John Henry stared in awe at this frail man wearing stained flannel pajamas and black socks with a blue stripe along the toes like his dad's and imagined him walking out from the rubble of a plane crash, not once, not twice, but three times. This man wasn't just a hero. He was a hero three times over. Lucky Strike.

"I'll tell you something about heroes, son," said the man quietly staring out into the distance like he wasn't really talking to John Henry. "There's heroes all around you. Closer than you think. You think a hero is somebody who risks his life?" he asked. John Henry nodded. "I guess maybe Webster's dictionary would say the same thing. But I've lived long enough and known enough heroes to know that it goes deeper than that, Son. There's plenty of heroes out there that's seen their moment of glory. Been paid tribute with medals and articles and books written about 'em. But what about the others? There's another kind of hero out there."

The man pointed out the window towards the center of Cedar Grove. "There's people out there right now. Maybe they haven't written the great American novel, or jumped out of a burning building, or brought a stadium full of people to their feet. Maybe they didn't risk their lives or overcome great obstacles like we're taught heroes should do. But what about the others out there? What word do we have for them? Maybe that's the problem. Maybe we don't think about them enough. Don't they get credit too?"

"Herman Simms, who mows the grass out here every week for example," said Lucky Strike. "Did you know he don't even get paid to do that? Just does it out of the kindness of his heart. That lady over there in the red dress. She comes every Sunday afternoon to do a daily devotional with whoever wants to hear it. Never misses a Sunday, not even on holidays. Don't tell me she don't have anything better to do.

"Take Andrew over there working at the desk. Did you know he goes home every day after work and takes care of his father? Feeds him, bathes him, changes him, reads to him, and sings his favorite songs with him. He gets up in the morning and his sister comes to take over so he can go to work. When little Percy Wintergreen took sick Pastor Isaiah spent the entire weekend in the hospital waiting room just to sit with his Nana. And when Booker Diggs's back went out, Luther Hawkins mowed his grass for him without even telling anybody he was gonna do it. And the ladies over at church cooked him meals in shifts."

"There's people who might not have had the chance to serve their country, but they're out there serving their neighbors, and God, and some of 'em doing it every single day. So, Son, don't go through your life so busy looking for heroes that you miss the ones staring you right in the face. The ones that matter most. You write your paper, Son. Use me if you see fit. But I had my moment of glory. I got my medal, I've had my moment. Maybe you might want to give someone else theirs."

John Henry debated for a long time. He knew Lucky Strike would win him that contest. But he couldn't help thinking about what Lucky said. And then he'd think about that bike. It was such a good prize. But the more he thought about it the more John Henry realized life isn't always about getting the prize. And John Henry grew a little bit bigger that day. Not in height but in heart. And he wrote his paper on heroes. Not one word about Lucky Strike. He figured he probably broke the rules cause he didn't write about one hero, he couldn't. The more he wrote the more he thought about. His town was just full of 'em. As he mailed in his contest entry he sighed and thought maybe one day there'd be another opportunity for that bike.

John Henry didn't win the contest. The judges gave the prize to a kid in Buncombe County who wrote in about his grandfather who was an Admiral. It was a good choice. John Henry got an honorable mention but no bike. And a reporter read his story on the TV news that night – a story about a little kid from Cedar Grove and the heroes in his town. It was a really neat story. But nobody saw it, including John Henry, 'cause they were all over at Old Man Byerly's place. That was the night it flooded and everybody pitched in to help. The whole town was there. They all missed hearing their moments of glory. Oh well, I guess that's the thing about heroes.

Salt and Pepper

Mamma and Daddy collected salt and pepper shakers. Spent most of their married lives traveling the world over in search of the perfect set. Never did find it. But they had hundreds of almost perfects. Ceramic pigs with curly tails. Porcelain kitties with red lips. White milky unicorns with gold horns. Pewter, wood, brass, brushed gold, and plastic. Speckled cows with pink udders. No matter what the flea market, antique show, or flea-ridden hotel up the coast, there was always a set they couldn't pass up. "Daddy," Mamma would say, "this is gonna worth a lot of money someday."

"Mamma," Daddy would say, "this is a deal. Get out the charge card." Too bad they never used salt or pepper. Didn't matter. To them it was a worthwhile monetary investment. They was saving up for their future, despite our urging them to invest their life savings into something more lucrative like savings bonds or one of them CDs. But they wouldn't listen. 'Cause other than the good Lord, they saw nothing better to put their faith in than a bona fide genuine original one and only hand carved set of wooden Easter bunny shakers. Or the fifty-year-old antiquated set of dark-haired ladies wearing hula skirts. Or that set that when put together made a donkey, salt being the head, and pepper being the rear.

Much to everyone's disbelief Mamma and Daddy remembered exactly where they bought every set of shakers, how much they cost, and their predicted value in twenty years, at least in their opinion anyway. It was the favorite pastime when company come. To have them pick up a set, any set. Mamma 'n Daddy wouldn't even have to be in the same room. All you had to do was call out "Dancing China Women" and Mamma'd say, "1942 Gas Station Gift Shop on Route 29."

Daddy'd say, "45 cents for the set."

Mamma'd say, "Must be worth at least $1.25 today."

Daddy'd say, "Yep, that was a deal."

We grew up thinking everybody's mamma and daddy collected salt and pepper shakers. That it was normal to open up your medicine cabinet and see a smiling clown staring back at you beside your floss. Didn't everybody have matching shark shakers from Myrtle Beach?

But as we grew older and ventured out to other friends' houses and only saw one set in the whole entire house, we realized the embarrassing truth. Especially when we'd have yard sales over at the church and Mamma would donate twenty-five sets of salt and pepper shakers and stand behind the table proudly explaining to each new owner the history behind it and what it would be worth someday.

As we became teenagers we thought it was just another one of those funny stupid things parents did and brought our friends over to see. Go ahead, we'd say. Put 'em to the test. Pick a shaker, any shaker. And the scrawny kid in braces would smile nervously and pick up a set of Elvises wearing blue suede shoes. "1984 Cracker Barrel gift shop in Minnesota," said Mamma. "He's still alive, you know."

"$4.00 marked 25% percent off," Daddy would say with pride. "But got to be worth at least twice that now."   Worked every time.

As we grew to be adults we thought it was cute. "How sweet," we'd say with a condescending smile, patting them on the back like well-behaved puppies. But at some point it turned the corner into not so cute. And it wasn't funny and it wasn't sweet. It was pathetic. We were worried about their state of mental being. Or maybe deep down we were worried that we were looking at ourselves one day and if there was a way we could stop it now, then perhaps we could change the path of destiny. We went to great lengths trying to convince our parents that it is not wise to lay your entire future at the feet of a porcelain pig wearing an apron.

The older our parents got, the smaller the house got on account of having to build more and more cabinets and shelves to hold all them salt 'n pepper shakers. Felt like the walls were closing in on that miniature fun house.

And then one day Mamma and Daddy were sitting in the den reading the paper when clear out of nowhere one of them "what if" moments hit 'em in the face like a splash of cold water. What if they were wrong? What if something happened in the economy and come time to cash in they weren't worth nothing?

Well, crazier things had happened. And after much prayerful thought they made the decision to cash in all them shakers. We couldn't have been more pleased and immediately offered to help for two reasons. One, Mamma and Daddy wouldn't know the first place to go looking for a buyer. And two, we simply couldn't bear the thought of what would happen when they found out that we'd been right all along and those salt and pepper shakers weren't even worth the salt and pepper to fill them up. So we found a local junk dealer who basically agreed to take the shakers off our hands. Then we told Mamma and Daddy what a great deal we got and gave them the money we had secretly pitched in together to come up with and no one was the wiser. Mamma and Daddy would never have to know that we really bought all them salt and pepper shakers. "Just think," Mamma told us as we handed her the check, "this'll be your inheritance one day."

When it come time for Mamma and Daddy to start packing 'em up we came along to help knowing it wasn't gonna be easy for Mamma and Daddy and to make sure none of those shakers got held back in a moment of weakness. Took 'em weeks to wrap up all them shakers cause each time they picked up a set they reminisced about where it was purchased, what particular Denny's they'd eaten at along the way, and which kid it was threw up in the parking lot. Which set was purchased the day each of us was born. Cowboys for the year the younger one wanted to be John Wayne when he grew up. The little kitty with the graduation cap. The birthday bears wearing party hats. Jesus with outstretched hands for the year we were baptized. It was like they were packing up their whole lives as each box closed on a Statue of Liberty or a deluxe edition Beatle. And when the man come to pick up the collection, well, it felt like a funeral. And in a way it was. We stood there on the corner, some of us with tears in our eyes, watching that rickety old truck disappear around the corner, taking with it a whole lifetime of treasured memories. Our memories – memories that wouldn't mean a thing to anyone else.

Mamma cried for weeks. Daddy puttered around the house in circles with no direction. No pigs to dust. No wood to polish. Sometimes you'd catch him standing in a bedroom staring at the empty shelves as if trying to will back his beloved friends. We hadn't expected them to take it so hard so we bought them a gift to brighten things up. A big screen TV. Not only was it their first TV set, but a big screen TV set at that. Mamma and Daddy forgot all their troubles while Daddy watched *How the West was Won* in such silent wide-eyed wonder that we had to keep checking his pulse. And Mamma almost swooned in her easy chair when she got to see Billy Graham speak for the first time in her life. Oh, she loved her radio, but seeing that man sitting in her living room larger than life, well, she almost couldn't catch her breath.

We patted ourselves on the back for a job well done, for having secured our parents' future. What would they do without us? But that ain't the end of the story. I'm afraid this ain't one of your happy-ever-after kind of stories, least not from where we sat. But I guess it depends on whose chair you're sitting in. In our eyes it was a hair's breath away from disaster when word spread that Mamma and Daddy had stumbled upon a new investment opportunity. Without our knowing. Without our input and financial assistance.

But from Mamma and Daddy's eyes it was nothing short of divine intervention when they was surfing the channels on that big screen TV we give 'em and saw the most beautiful thing they'd ever laid eyes on. The shopping channel. And lo and behold bless God and the angels for what should be on that particular day and that particular moment but an auction. And what were they auctioning off? Salt and pepper shakers. "Not just any salt and pepper shakers," said the announcer holding up a matching set of cut glass roosters. "But antique Retro shakers dating back as far as the 20's. Folks, you can't find this stuff today. I'd suggest you call in right now and put your money down. We may never see antiques like this again."

Yep, salt and pepper shakers, of all things. The very same salt and pepper shakers Mamma and Daddy had spent their whole lives and souls collecting. Daddy turns to Mamma. Mamma turns to Daddy and with the unanimous unspoken connection often acquired through sixty years of marriage they nodded. "Mamma," said Daddy in that serious look he reserved for deacon meetings and funerals, "that looks like a deal. Let's buy them all. Get out the charge card." And in the privacy of their living room, in a three-minute phone conversation, Mamma and Daddy made a purchase. Bought every one. Paid twice what they had supposedly sold them shakers for. But way they saw it, it was a worthwhile monetary investment. And they had us to thank.

We couldn't help but wonder who was more foolish, Mamma and Daddy for investing in salt and pepper shakers, or us, for standing in the way of destiny. I'm reminded of it often. Every time I walk into my dining room and look at the top shelf of the china cabinet where the light shines on the ceramic bluebirds. Every time someone visits and stops to admire the brushed gold set of wise men or the Elvises with blue suede shoes. And my kids proudly tell their friends that I know where every set was purchased and how much it cost. And they laugh when I say, "Yep, it's gonna be worth a lot of money someday." It's already worth more than they'll ever know.

Wretched Gretchen

Sometimes you don't see God's hand in things and sometimes you do. And sometimes the only ones who see it are the ones who's looking. I was twelve years old the year I saw God at work in our town. Twelve years old when I realized that the whole world did not revolve around Cedar Grove with its two stoplights total and one-half of a fast-food restaurant. Maybe it was television. Maybe it was books or movies. Something showed me a world outside our town that was faster, that had more exciting stuff in it. A world that suddenly I dreamed about living in. And I would stare down that road leading out of Cedar Grove and picture myself on it. With a suitcase in one hand and a guitar in the other like Maria in *The Sound of Music*. But I couldn't sing or play the guitar. Minor details. I was twelve when I decided to be a writer and started dreaming of a better life. Of a place where people made things happen — left their marks on the world. Great American novels didn't come from Cedar Grove and neither would mine. It was the year I started thinking bigger.

It was the year that folks in Cedar Grove slipped away from God. Only I didn't know it then. And they didn't either. Some things you just don't see coming. They happen so slow that you don't notice it. Like that leak we had in the basement behind the furnace; and it was my job to keep the bucket emptied till Daddy could fix it. It was such a tiny leak I didn't think it was any big deal and figured it'd take years to fill that bucket and so I never checked it. Then one day that bucket filled up and overflowed into Mamma's magazines. Got my butt whupped for that one. All on account of a tiny leak. Maybe that's what happened in Cedar Grove that year. Folks didn't notice the leak till it was running over. And even then I still ain't sure they noticed it.

It was the year we got that new baptismal pool and suddenly all these folks were becoming reborn so's they could get dunked in it. And it was the year I first saw Wretched Gretchen up close. Twelve years old before I saw for myself the reason folks didn't look her in the eye. It was hard to, for starters, 'cause she had wild eyes that rolled all over the place and never really focused straight on you.

She had the makings of a beard and craters in her face like a piece of old Swiss cheese. Her teeth looked like a dried out old corncob halfway eaten. I was kind of scared when she sat beside me. Mamma says there's no reason to be scared of Gretchen, bless her heart. Folks said that a lot whenever they talked about Gretchen. Oh, she must be freezing with no coat, bless her heart. Oh, she's going through the trash again, bless her heart. For the longest time I thought that was her last name: Gretchen Bless Her Heart.

She had painted on eyebrows in this reddish color that made a thin arch over her bulging eyes. I could see why the boys called her toad and sang that song about her on the playground.

Wretched Gretchen, Wretched Gretchen,
Seein' her makes you feel like retchin'
Better not let her breathe on you
You might become a Gretchen too.

She had on a sweater that I thought looked a lot like one my daddy used to have. Probably was. Gretchen was always wearing stuff she got from Goodwill or at the soup kitchen box of free clothes. Being as Cedar Grove was so small we usually recognized something she was wearing.

Gretchen lived in one of them mill houses at the edge of town. It had a red door and a bunch of cats that was always curling around the posts and peeking at you from behind curtains.

So, anyway, this all happened the year I was twelve. The year Cedar Grove got all swept up in that time capsule craziness, as Mamma called it. I think it was Aunt Bitsy who started it all when she saw on this talk show how somewhere out west they dug up this time capsule from forty-two years before that a little kid had buried in his back yard. Found it when they was putting in a swimming pool and everybody was acting like they'd found a dinosaur's hindquarters or something. Seemed kind of dumb to me. All it had in it was a quarter, and a yo yo, a watch, and something wrapped up like candy but it was all molded.

Then somebody gets the idea that Cedar Grove should do a time capsule and Mayor Clinard thought it would be great for publicity and they decided to bury it in back of the Post Office since there wasn't any chance of a swimming pool being put out there. And Skeeter said they could use his digger and Booker said he'd organize the work crew and Beauregard DuBerry said they ought to have a celebration picnic on the day they buried it and that his wife Porticia could plan it, what with her having skills in that area. And Aunt Vyrnetta said she'd sing and next thing you know the ladies was tripping over each other in their hurry to get home and start planning what they were gonna cook. And that's how it all got started.

Mayor Clinard scheduled a meeting at the town hall to discuss what would go in the box and the only thing they agreed on was that it had to be a box filled with things that represented Cedar Grove. That was the only thing they agreed on. I could hear 'em all arguing in my bed that night long after dark 'cause my window was open and our house was only spitting distance from town hall. Seems folks had different ideas on what represented Cedar Grove.

Ray Jean wanted one of her diner menus to go in there on account of that diner was the oldest running restaurant in Cedar Grove and her corned beef and cabbage special was good enough to go down in history if anything was. Aunt Vyrnetta wanted to put one of her special occasion wigs in there 'cause how neat that would be for folks to find it long after she was gone and realize it belonged to the famous singer from Cedar Grove. Aunt Vyrnetta was not a famous singer but was quite sure that one day she would be. If you could hear her sing you'd understand why Mamma said that woman was delusional.

Aunt Bitsy wanted to put a packet of that artificial sweetener in there with a note that said, "See, I told you one day it was gonna kill us all." And Fernetta Stutts replied by saying that if artificial sweetener was gonna eventually kill us all, as Aunt Bitsy was so bound and determined to believe, then who would be alive to read the note? And that's how Fernetta and Aunt Bitsy come to be on non-speaking terms.

Granny Jean wanted to put her third husband's cufflinks in there with a note saying, "Don't ever marry a Munsen; you're just asking for misery," which offended Sara Hardison, who said she had some Munsens in her family somewhere down the line and that's how Granny and Sara stopped speaking.

Mildred Jenkins thought they should put a church hymnal in there, to which Cleetus Harley replied that was dumb 'cause even if the thing wasn't found for a hundred years it wouldn't be that big a deal 'cause they'd probably still be singing them same old tired church songs. And Mildred told him he was blasphemizing and Cleetus accused her of being judgmental and that's how Mildred and Cleetus come to be on non-speaking terms. And the meeting got real quiet after a while 'cause nobody was speaking.

Finally Mayor Clinard said he'd hold a contest and anybody who wanted to could enter an item as a candidate for the box and then the whole town would vote and the winners would get their stuff to go in the box. And I tell you what, folks become obsessed with that time capsule craziness. It was like they were getting on Star Search or something. They were giving way more attention than it deserved according to my mamma who said she wasn't gonna enter anything in that contest and just add to the nonsense. But I saw her holding one of Mammy Bee's china tea cups up to the light and reviewing it from all angles and I knew what she was thinking even if she didn't admit it.

I had already picked out what I was gonna enter for the contest — a picture of the Cedar Grove Baptist Church Christmas Pageant from three years ago. It just about had the whole town in it. I couldn't think of anything better to represent our town than that and thought maybe about writing a story about it but decided better. Great American novels didn't have angels wearing wings made out of coat hangers covered in queen-sized pantyhose and wise men leading dogs with makeshift humps on their backs to look like camels.

Folks spent the next two weeks getting ready for that contest. Norm Pascal made a flute out of a branch from a tree his father planted when he was a kid. Beautiful hand carved flute. It didn't work 'cause Norm didn't know how to make a flute and wasn't one for reading instructions so he had improvised. It was about two feet longer than the time capsule box but he was gonna enter it anyway. Booker Diggs spent hours trying to decide which one of his poems to enter in the contest, which raised immediate objection from the churchgoing folks who were all too well acquainted with Booker's heartfelt poems on fishing and beer.

My friend Timmy Weathersby was gonna enter his shark's tooth from Myrtle Beach and Luther was gonna put some grape bubblegum in there since it was his favorite and John Henry was planning something underhanded, being the troublemaker that he was, but somebody caught wind and shuffled him off to his cousin's for a last minute visit so he couldn't ruin the whole thing, which was probably a good idea since folks still hadn't quite gotten over that incident with Miss Phoebe's poodle and the hair dye.

Myrlene, Vyrlene, and Shirlene Smith were gonna enter pink sponge rollers from *Myrlene, Vyrlene, and Shirlene's House of Beauty* to show folks of the future what women in the olden days had to go through to get good hair. And folks were digging through closets and attics to find items that represented their most worthwhile achievements in life. There were letter sweaters and softball trophies, paycheck stubs and certificates of merit. Songs on cassette tapes, diplomas, and bronzed baby shoes. There was even a purple heart in there and after that people figured the contest was good as over — couldn't nothing compete with a purple heart. Come the day of that picnic the contest table was piled high with items that represented Cedar Grove and to strangers passing through would have probably screamed out yard sale if anything ever did.

There wasn't a person in town that missed that picnic, including Wretched Gretchen, who I hadn't seen since the whole time capsule business started. She looked the same. Still wearing that olive sweater with the holes in it and them work boots that didn't have the laces in one shoe while the rest of us were running around in shorts and tank tops. I decided Gretchen was just plain out weird and that was all there was to it. Weird Wretched Gretchen, bless her heart.

Mayor Clinard gave a touching speech about the history of Cedar Grove which didn't take long. Then he talked about the time capsule and how it represented our town and told us all a bunch of stuff we already knew about the time capsule concept but I guess he was repeating it for the reporter sitting in the back row with his photographer who kept snapping photographs of Aunt Vyrnetta in her low cut pink sequined pants suit. Aunt Vyrnetta had a pink wig to match piled up on her head and covered with little gold butterflies. But I don't think it was them butterflies that photographer was lookin' at when Aunt Vyrnetta sang *Isn't It Romantic* and about made us all throw up. Good thing she sang before lunch.

People were so excited about the contest they didn't mind when Herschel found that dead fly in the potato salad and pitched a fit at his wife Fran for not putting a cover on it like he told her. Skeeter yelled out to Herschel that there was no reason to fly off the handle and Booker laughed so hard he fell out of his chair. Herschel usually had a quick temper but not that day. He even laughed about it. I guess 'cause he was sure he'd win him the contest with his basketball scholarship letter he'd held on to since high school. He never went to college on account of his daddy getting sick and them needing his help at the farm. But he figured that letter was worthy of being remembered as anything.

The contest was held after everything was cleared away from the picnic and the little ones had a chance to run around amuck as Mamma called it and the older folks had a chance to let their food settle. The Fellowship Fiddlers played some music but they weren't real good 'cause that was their first official gig, even though they weren't getting paid. And some of the folks got up to clog 'cause you can't have fiddling with out clogging. Just ain't natural, as my daddy would say. And folks was clear tearing up the floor, as Nana Hawkins put it, which upset some of the Baptists but even they put their opinions aside for the time being on account of the whole time capsule nonsense, as Mamma was still calling it.

Just as the sun was thinking about setting, Mayor Clinard announced that it was time to review the entries and the band stopped playing and the kids stopped screaming and the adult folk stopped talking and a hush settled over Cedar Grove — a hush that would never happen twice in that town. And they waited. Waited and watched with anticipation as Mayor Clinard held up every item displayed on the tables. Took four long banquet tables to hold all the stuff folks was entering and there was everything from photo albums to jewelry to toys — even a dog bone hanging in the mix. I looked at all the stuff piled on the tables and thought about how it was supposed to represent my town. I thought it surely did at that. Looked like a junk sale display table. Nothing exciting, 'cause like I told you, exciting stuff doesn't come from Cedar Grove. Now you follow that road out of town and see what their time capsule's got in it. I'd bet it would put ours to shame.

Wretched Gretchen was sitting under a willow tree with a grocery bag on her lap during all the festivities. Just a plain old garbage bag I figured she brought to take home what food was left over. Nobody sat beside her except for one of her cats curled up against her leg. It was an orange cat, not the black one missing an eye that always followed her around. Come to think of it, I hadn't seen that mangy old one-eyed cat in a long time. Maybe even since last summer. I wondered if it died. Probably did. I wondered if anybody knew Wretched Gretchen's cat died. When my cat Tinks died, I cried for a week straight. Still sometimes I can cry if I think about her real hard. She died on my birthday. I remember 'cause having your cat die on your birthday is something you ain't likely to forget. I was wearing my new blue dress with the daisies stitched around the collar. That was the saddest day I ever knew.

I wondered when Gretchen's birthday was. Never heard of anybody giving her a present or having a party for her or nothing. Mamma said people like Gretchen like to be left to their peace. I couldn't imagine being left to my peace on my own birthday. Just some occasions ain't the same when you spend 'em alone.

It wasn't till Mayor Clinard got to the end of the last table that Gretchen stood up and shuffled over to it and laid her bag on the end of it, and turned around and walked off. Didn't even wait to see if she was gonna win. Just her and that orange cat bouncing around her feet. Mayor Clinard peered into her bag and we all held our breaths. "Probably a skull," Luther whispered. And the way he said it made me like him a little bit less that day. "Maybe it's her teeth," he whispered and the other boys laughed. I didn't laugh.

Mayor Clinard reached into the bag slowly like maybe he was half expecting it to be a dead animal or something. "Go ahead Clinard, you'll still have your other arm," someone called out from the back and the adults laughed. I liked them a little bit less that day too. Even my mamma laughed.

Mayor pulled a bundle of cloth out of the bag. Folks started to move in for a closer look. I guess they had to see for themselves what Wretched Gretchen felt was her mark on the world. And there it was. Mayor didn't say anything, just laid it out on the table and everybody stared as more and more folks come up to see.

It was a quilt. Not the kind of quilt you'd see hanging in Sally's Sewing Shop real high up so's you won't spill your soda on it or nothing. It was different 'cause it didn't have matching pieces like the kind in the store. But it was beautiful. Nana Hawkins inspected it closely and informed us all that it had been stitched by hand. The threads weren't all the same color but the stitching was perfect. And in the corner were initials stitched just as clear as can be – WG. "Who's WG?" someone asked. They thought about it but couldn't for the life of 'em figure out anybody with them initials. Somebody suggested maybe it was a distant relative but it just didn't figure into things.

"It's Wretched Gretchen," I said quietly thinking nobody heard me but they did.

"Wretched Gretchen?" Mayor Clinard repeated. I nodded.

"It's what some of the kids call her," I said in a tiny voice. How did Wretched Gretchen know that's what we called her? I wondered. And then I noticed a scrap of fabric near the top of that quilt– blue with daisies stitched on it. "Mamma, that's my birthday dress," I said pointing at the square while Mamma shook her head.

"No dear, it probably just looks like it."

"Wait a minute," said Pastor Isaiah picking up a corner of the quilt and studying it closely. "That's a piece from my preaching robe – the first one I ever preached a real sermon in. But I got rid of that years ago." Amanda Brice let out a tiny gasp and picked up another corner of the quilt while a tear rolled down her cheek.

"That's my baby's," she whispered and tears kept falling down her cheeks. Amanda Brice's baby had lived for three days.

Born with a hole in her heart. That faded yellow scrap was a piece of the blanket they brought her home in that day. Amanda told her husband to get rid of it and he had given it to Goodwill.

"Charlie, isn't that your daddy's military uniform?" Mertice whispered and pointed.

"And that's the plaid shirt I had on when I won the spelling bee," said Tater nodding emphatically. And suddenly everybody was noticing pieces that had once belonged to them. Not just ordinary pieces either but from important moments like weddings and funerals, baptisms, and the dress that Maybelle Simms had on when they found her that day in the woods, and the flag that had hung out front of the Post Office for years until John Henry accidentally shot it with his BB gun during a game of war and they had to get a new one.

I couldn't stop looking at the piece that was blue with the daisies on it. My birthday dress. The day my cat died. It was like Wretched Gretchen knew it was the saddest day of my life. Like Wretched Gretchen knew what all our important days were. And it was quiet out there under that willow tree as people stood under the setting sun while the breeze blew across the surface of that quilt — everybody lost in their memories.

There was no vote that day 'cause suddenly nothing else seemed as important as that quilt. Wretched Gretchen had taught us that it wasn't accomplishments or achievements or things that represented our town. It was the people. And the love they showed each other when it counted. We'd been so caught up in the legacy that we were gonna leave the world that we forgot what was important. Little by little until it was running over.

And then Pastor Isaiah pointed out the scrap in the very center of the quilt. It was a bright green color that surely nobody would ever pick to wear. But it was thicker than a shirt or a dress. It was more like fabric off of furniture, like would go on a sofa or a chair. Heads started to nod as they recognized it. It was the fabric from the church pews — right there in the center of the quilt — a piece of our church. Cedar Grove – the town built around a Baptist church. It was like Wretched Gretchen was telling us that we had forgotten about God.

Suddenly the rest of the stuff piled on that table was just stuff. Not as important as it was only five minutes before. Staring at that quilt, folks saw what their town represented. Not what, but who. It wasn't about what they'd done, but who had been there to share it. And that scrap in the middle reminded them that it's not about the mark you leave on the world but the mark you leave on God. And they'd forgotten that. Slipped away from them little by little. But like God is so good at doing, he sent a reminder we called Wretched Gretchen.

That was the day I learned that it's not about what you leave behind or what others say about you after you're gone, but what God says. Life isn't about achievements or goals reached. It's about love. Unconditional love. The kind of love Gretchen showed to people who didn't love her back. Kind of like God. From that day on whenever I saw Wretched Gretchen, I didn't see flaws. I saw beauty. And a quilt that taught a town to love.

> *Romans 14:9-12 "Christ died and rose again for this very purpose, so that he might be Lord of those who are alive and of those who have died. [10] So why do you condemn another Christian? Why do you look down on another Christian? Remember, each of us will stand personally before the judgment seat of God. [11] For the Scriptures say, 'As surely as I live,' says the Lord, 'every knee will bow to me and every tongue will confess allegiance to God.'[12] Yes, each of us will have to give a personal account to God."*

The Pressure Washer

Arlis Jones had a weakness for power tools and fixing things. To him it wasn't a matter of the tool fitting the work but making the work fit the tool. And Arlis was a genius at finding any reason to use a tool. Like when the Christmas tree branches were uneven.

"Easy," said Arlis, who sawed off the offending branches, drilled new holes in the empty gaps, filled the holes with the sawed off branches, used industrial strength glue to hold it in place, and *voila*. Problem solved.

Arlis decided to regrout the bathroom, or better to say Arlis bought a heavy duty caulking gun and then decided to regrout the bathroom and used so much industrial strength rubber-like caulking that he covered just about every surface in that bathroom to the point you could bounce china tea cups off the walls and they wouldn't break. Arlis knew 'cause he and Earl tested it.

Arlis found a way to add "juice" to the vacuum cleaner and that was the last they saw of the guinea pig and Ray Jean's sponge rollers. The blender now works at such a high speed that no one's allowed to use it for fear of losing a limb. And last time Ray Jean used her new garden tub with the jet massagers, well, the bruises lasted for days.

Arlis got a cement mixer and made his own patio, and walkway, and basketball court, and driveway extension, and garden stones, and a bench, and was just about to widen the front sidewalk when the city caught wind of it and ended his cement mixing days forever.

Arlis built a lovely deck with built-in benches, and a trellis, and an overhang, and a picnic table, and was gonna build him an Adirondack chair but couldn't ever spell it well enough to find the specs on the internet and got sidetracked into buying a power mower that was too big to fit in his own shed and he had to get a storage unit for it.

Arlis had a dead tree stump he needed to remove and figured to heck with tree stump remover, what good could anything be in a bottle that small, and used dynamite instead.

Just about wiped his street off the map. Cleared every tree and unearthed the chain-link fence, which he figured needed upgrading anyway. But the stump was gone.

Arlis near about drove Ray Jean crazy but the real trouble didn't start until Arlis Jones bought himself a pressure washer. Arlis had never used a pressure washer and neither had anybody he knew, which added to its appeal. Of course there might be a reason you don't find a pressure washer sitting inside every garage. Starting with the price. Ray Jean still don't know it yet but Arlis could have sent a kid over to the community college for what he paid for that washer. But Arlis had taken one look at the big black bold words HIGH POWER and there was no turning back. Before Arlis even left *Skeeter's Hardware* he'd already come up with a list of things he was gonna wash, starting with the deck.

Arlis's pressure washer might have come with instructions but if it did Arlis didn't see 'em. He wasn't much for reading directions anyway. Just point him to the on button and he could take it from there. He was in control. But with the pressure washer, well, he'd met his match. 'Cause with a pressure washer control is not always easily determined. Looking back, it's safe to say that there was not one moment when Arlis was in control of that pressure washer, not even when it was still sitting on that shelf in the store.

Ray Jean did not see the obvious beauty and value of owning a pressure washer. Good thing she didn't know the investment involved. She had but one comment to make. "You ruin my roses and you are sleeping in the shed the whole summer." Ray Jean had put many hours, sweat, and tears into that rose garden. She fiercely protected it like a mother bear would her cubs. You may wonder what a rose garden would have to do with pressure washing. Surely Arlis wasn't dumb enough to pressure wash the roses.

So Arlis decides to pressure wash the deck on a cool spring Saturday morning when bluebirds chattered happily in the trees and the flowers danced back and forth under the warm sun. Ray Jean was getting a little sun on the patio while Otis slept peacefully at her feet snoring as only a dog can. Everything was tranquil and lovely and the smell of honeysuckles, nature's deodorizer, drifted in the air. You probably feel like you're in one of those scenes in a horror movie where the lovely blonde actress smiles at herself in the bathroom mirror, breathes in deeply reflecting on life as seen from a steamy room that houses the commode, and steps into the shower while you scream at the TV, "Nooooooo! Don't get in the shower! He's hiding behind the door!"

I think it's what they call foreshadowing, giving you the sense that something is gonna happen and only you know about it so far. In which case, you are most definitely correct. This pleasant spring morning has no idea what terror awaits in the hands of that pressure washing madman.

Arlis's famous last words were, "Look out honey, wouldn't want to spray you." Words which were drowned out (literally) by the opening spray of that pressure washer that roared into that peaceful spring morning like an uncaged beast. It's hard to say whether Arlis was holding the pressure washer or whether the pressure washer was holding Arlis the way he was flipping around that back yard like a piñata, that hose slapping him left to right so fast he looked like a rubber gummy worm.

Ray Jean screamed as the jet stream of high pressure water slammed her out of the chair and up against the storage shed wall with her legs dangling like a rag doll while water sprayed the side of that shed with such force it sounded like rapid firing bullets. Then it turned to feast on some other unsuspecting creature like Mildred Jenkins, the elderly lady from next door, who was peeking over the fence to see what all the commotion was about when a blast of water shot her little hat with plastic daisies on it clear off her head and into the next yard and Mildred hit the ground just like she's seen 'em do in the movies.

Harvey Diggs picked the wrong moment to deliver that fruitcake to Ray Jean like his wife asked him to and, when he couldn't get an answer up front, walked around to the back thinking he was walking in on some kind of serious domestic violence. He called out to Arlis and that angry pressure washer turned its head and set its eyes on Harvey Diggs who opened his mouth wide in terror and, well, let's just say that was the end of that fruitcake and Harvey's hair piece which was now plastered to the side of Arlis's Buick like back country road kill. It was only by the grace of God that Arlis managed to turn the thing off. The slain beast lay there limp on the grass and they all stood there panting heavily while the rest of the neighborhood come running up to survey the damage. Jaws dropped one after the other as they stared in awe at how much damage could be done in so short a time.

"What were you thinking, Arlis?" asked Mildred.

"I was pressure washing the deck," Arlis replied, still in shock.

"Well," said Ned. "Looks like you did some pressure washing."

A lot of home improvements were made that day if you want to call them that. Arlis's deck is now the size of a picnic table. The side wall of the shed is missing, last seen hurtling in the direction of the public pool. The house used to have shutters and now it don't. Used to not have sunlights and now it does. The backyard looks like a war zone with three dead squirrels, a headless baby doll, a tricycle whose handlebars have blown away, and the tire rim of a ten-speed bike lodged up in a tree. The tomatoes and cucumbers are gone, including the sticks to hold 'em up. The shrubs are flattened and the dog is still missing. And the worst thing, Ray Jean's roses. Destroyed. Death due to over watering according to the landscaping guy. Talk about your understatements.

Now Arlis has a bed in the shed. Just him and his tools. He's had lots of time to think about the incident out in that shed. And he's realized something very valuable. There must be a way to reduce the power on that washer. Maybe if he just tweaked it a little.

Jesus Comes to Visit

Did I ever tell you about the time Cedar Grove was convinced that Jesus was coming for Christmas? Where John Henry Junior was from, Christmas started about thirty seconds after the last turkey bone was licked clean at Thanksgiving. Hanging icicle lights, decorated trees, waving Santas, carolers, pageants, sugar plum fairies — Cedar Grove did it all with quite a flourish. Being a town built around a Baptist Church, folks knew full well the meaning of Christmas. But sometimes even the most well-meaning of folks can lose sight of the big picture without even knowing it and the Christmas message gets lost somewhere in between spraying the front windows with artificial snow and getting Uncle Herschel's underwear size. Maybe that's what happened in Cedar Grove and that's why there's a story to tell. But it all started with Grandma Nelly and another one of her famous premonitions.

It was the year after the fruitcake incident and the year before Cedar Grove got swindled by that traveling Bible salesman in the plaid suit. It was the last year Grandma Nelly was alive. Eighty-nine years old she was, and the oldest living inhabitant of Cedar Grove. But that was not her claim to fame. What folks will always remember about Grandma Nelly was that she saw things before they happened. Scenes played out in her head like a movie. She had an aura about her as folks used to say.

Grandma Nelly had one of her famous premonitions during the Thanksgiving meal that year that Jesus was coming down to pay a visit to Cedar Grove. Yep, that's right, the good Lord Himself coming to a town so small that you could throw a rock from one end to the other. Word of the premonition spread like a brush fire. Folks did not know what to make of it. In Cedar Grove, way they saw it, if it wasn't written in the Bible, it wasn't true. And wasn't anybody could remember reading about Jesus coming back, 'cept for the real thing, and surely he wouldn't choose Cedar Grove for his second coming!

So folks laughed it off and went on about their business or at least tried to anyway. But they couldn't forget about it. Grandma Nelly had never been wrong before. They had to admit that. But there was always a first time. And she was convinced her premonition would come true. Said it was plain and clear as a premonition can be. But then she was eighty-nine after all, it was about time for her to start losing control of her faculties. And folks went back and forth about it and over time, well, it didn't seem so funny anymore. I mean, after all, she did have an aura.

And the more they wondered and what if'd, the more folks started entertaining the thought. And once one or two entertained the thought, it turned into four and five until the majority of folks started believing it might happen, which was only a skip away from being convinced. And so that's how most of Cedar Grove come to believe that Jesus was coming for Christmas, which burdened Pastor Isaiah something fierce as he saw his town headed down a very bumpy road.

Pastor Isaiah loved his flock and spent great time fretting over its salvation, which he now considered to be in serious jeopardy ever since news of this blasphemous premonition. He knew that Jesus was not coming down to Cedar Grove for a visit. Problem was making his flock believe it without breaking their hearts in the process. After all, folks can get mighty offended when it comes to matters of the religious persuasion. He didn't have the first idea of how to fix the situation so he did what most Pastors would do. He prayed on it.

And while Pastor Isaiah fervently prayed for all the souls of Cedar Grove, his flock worked just as fervently making way for the Savior's arrival. There wasn't a person in that town who didn't hope that Jesus would be sitting at their table come Christmas supper.

"What will he look like?" someone asked Grandma Nelly who announced, much to their dismay, that Jesus would come in the form of something they see every day. Well, you can imagine the confusion this created as suddenly everything had the potential of being Jesus in disguise. Suddenly folks started taking a closer look at things like bushes, and lamp posts, and family pets, just in case.

"When will he get here?" someone asked. "Whose house will he stay at? How long will he be here for?" asked another. Grandma Nelly's only answer was that he was coming for

Christmas and she didn't know when, or for how long, or whose house he would stay at, or whether he liked his mashed potatoes skins on or skins off, and would folks quit bugging her about it for heaven's sake. She wasn't his agent!

So the holiday season in Cedar Grove took a turn from the usual flurry of activity on account of the arrival of Jesus was more important than the buy one get one free sale on wrapping paper at the grocery, or the holiday poinsettias fifty percent off. Clayton Birch finally got around to cleaning out his gutters like he'd been promising his wife for years. After all, what kind of impression would that make to their important guest, having dirty gutters and all. *Myrlene, Vyrlene, and Shirlene's House of Beauty* had to stay open till after dark what with all the womenfolk getting perms, highlights, and their nails done for the noteworthy occasion. And the streets of Cedar Grove had a thin layer of flour and sugar what with all the pie making and biscuit rolling as they all tried to outdo each other, knowing that even Jesus couldn't resist a homemade chicken pot pie.

The Cedar Grove Baptist Church Choir practiced an extra hour each week and Mrs. O'Henry, the first grade teacher at Cedar Grove Elementary, went to great pains to make sure every detail of Cedar Grove's Christmas Pageant was correct. After all, Jesus was gonna be their critic. As Christmas Eve approached, there was so much anticipatin' going on that it hung over the town like a fog.

Only one who paid no mind to all the commotion was John Henry's mamma, who did not give one second of serious thought to Grandma Nelly's premonition. She knew Jesus was not coming to visit Cedar Grove. That when he would come it would be for good and wouldn't nobody be able to foresee the good Lord's coming. And if folks continued such nonsense, the end times just might happen sooner than they think. And it would serve them right the way they carried on so. And she went about making her Christmas fruitcakes like she did every year without doing a single thing different. And come Christmas Eve, she sent John Henry Jr. out door to door to deliver the fruitcakes.

John Henry was amazed at all the fuss. Old Man Jake's whole yard was covered in blinking white lights strung through tree limbs and bushes. Mr. Hatcher had a real live nativity scene in his front yard and used his own wife and kids as the animals. His Aunt Vyrnetta answered the door wearing a long white sequined gown that had been hand-sewn and flown in from Italy. Kids were cleaning their rooms and women were mopping floors so clean you could lick off 'em. And when John Henry Jr. delivered the fruitcake to Old man Peterson, who was cleaning out his stables, why, John Henry swore he heard that old man call his new prize stallion the King of the Jews.

Pastor Isaiah was John Henry's last stop. It was late, but the Pastor was still up working on his Christmas sermon, surrounded by crumpled paper. He looked like he'd been chewed up and spit out. I guess that's what worrying about folks' souls will do to you. He had prayed and cried and cursed and prayed some more and still couldn't find the right words.

"Merry Christmas, Pastor Isaiah," said John Henry, handing him the last fruitcake that was rather smooshed on account of it was laying in the bottom of the box and John Henry had dropped it and it rolled down the front steps so it had a couple of leaves stuck to it. "Sorry, Pastor Isaiah. Guess it really is the thought that counts," he said with a smile and darted out the door for home.

The pastor stared with tired eyes at that lopsided fruitcake while the words rolled around in his head. The thought that counts. The thought that counts. And then it hit him like a freight train. He had been so focused on it that he couldn't see it. Of course, he exclaimed in excitement, praised the almighty God for answering his prayers, and began to write.

Come Christmas morning, a blanket of disappointment hung over the town. Jesus never came. Even though the Pastor knew it had been foolishness, it still made him sad. "My dear friends," he began. "I know that you have spent weeks waiting for the arrival of Jesus. I think that all of us at times find ourselves desperately wanting to believe something that's not going to happen. I know you are disappointed and you feel that it was all just a foolish whim. And until last night I would have agreed. And then I realized that I wasn't seeing the big picture. I knew Jesus wasn't coming for a visit, at least not like you were expecting him. That was always the truth. But I was so concerned about your false hope that I missed what was really happening. I was so caught up in how to prove you were wrong that I didn't even look for the good in it.

"I'm not talking about the preparations and hard work. I'm talking about something deeper. Something that lingered in the air and not the smell of warm apple pies but kindness, and love. I was too busy fretting over your mistakes that I didn't notice how you were changing. How you started overlooking your differences. Sam, I saw you help Horace change the tire on his tractor. Three weeks ago you would have rather had your right arm cut off than even walk on the same side of the street as him. Lottie, you stopped bickering over that tree limb hanging over your fence, and Erma, you finally stopped talking about that money your cousin over in Clayton borrowed and never returned. Nobody whispered about who didn't put any money in the collection plate, or who spent more money than they should have on that new car. Some of you living on hard times found anonymous gifts on your front porch, bills paid by unknown donors, front porches swept while you were away. Grudges were forgiven and enemies became friends.

"You started talking to God more and taking a good look at the way you lived your lives, reflecting on your sins, and asking Him to forgive you. The whole time you were looking for Jesus to sprout out of a bush or ride up to your front door, something beautiful was happening. You started living to please Jesus 'cause you weren't sure just when he would appear. And shouldn't we do that all the time? Shouldn't we spend every day of our lives doing things to please him?

"You were waiting for a special guest this Christmas, but I think you got something better than you were looking for, a lesson in how to live every day as if Jesus might walk through your front door. And don't think he doesn't see what you do.

"He may not be sitting at your dinner table enjoying your skins-on mashed potatoes, but he watched you sweep your neighbor's porch, and he watched you give to someone who needed it. And he heard every prayer you whispered and saw every tear you shed. So was it really all for nothing? I don't think so. It's the thought that really counts. So today let's celebrate Jesus' birth and praise God that he is coming back one day to stay. And I hope we'll all be ready. Amen."

Grandma Nelly died on Christmas morning while we were all sitting there in church. Just slipped out of this world quiet as you please, aura and all.

The Time Mamma Brought Lucas Diggs
Home for Christmas

Did I ever tell you about the time Mamma brought Lucas Diggs home for Christmas? It was that point in my life when I was convinced that Mamma's sole purpose was to make my life miserable. Okay, so I was a drama queen. Later I realized how little I really knew about my mamma. But I was right about one thing, Mamma did nothing in moderation. Especially Christmas.

It was Mamma who asked the annual holiday kick-off question, So, what does everybody want for Christmas? That was actually a rhetorical question (meaning she really wasn't waiting for an answer), 'cause Mamma got you what she wanted you to have. Like the year my brother John Henry got a second-hand pan flute 'cause Mamma liked the way it sounded on that commercial. He had asked for a bike.

Yep, that was Mamma. Strangers called her Mrs. Henry, other folks called her Suga. But to the rest of us, she was just Mamma, a sizeable woman with many folds, or pillows as she liked to call them, a giant laugh that rumbled from the bottom of her soul like thunder, and a heart to match. It's what folks in Cedar Grove still talk about today. That, and the time she picked Cleetus up by the seat of his pants and dumped him in the creek for smacking his wife's behind in public. You didn't mess with Mamma. In fact, there was only one person who ever got the better of her, but I'm afraid I'm rushing the story.

I had just turned eighteen that year and settled into the fact that I was too old to run away from home and too lazy to enlist, so I decided to make the most of my wretched situation by making everyone around me as miserable as I was. Sometimes teenage girls can be quite good at that. It was the year Uncle Pete decided to introduce the family to his new girlfriend Rochelle, who was a thirty-five-year-old underwear model for Sears, which in Pete's eyes was just the coolest thing in the world. Only Grandpa Horace had already had two heart attacks and they were all afraid that an underwear model just might be the final kick to his old ticker. It was the year Aunt Rose divorced her husband Maurice on account of him trying on her new lace panties and it was the year our next door neighbor Horace got sent off to the loony bin on account of him running around his backyard clucking like a chicken.

It was the year I had decided that, instead of going to college, I was gonna become one of them nude models, which my brothers found particularly revolting. It was the year Aunt Bitsy announced she wouldn't eat anything that had a mamma and would bring a soy turkey instead. And Uncle Frank wanted to know could he bring his new boss, Fritz, and since Fritz was a member of the Earth Church, could we please stay away from any religious conversation. It was the year John Henry had to help Mamma with the fruitcake project and share a bed with our cousin Donald, who drooled in his sleep like a busted pipe. When he wasn't wetting the bed, that is. And then, as if things couldn't get any worse, Mamma brought Lucas Diggs home for Christmas.

Lucas Diggs appeared to be about one meal short of starving. He couldn't have been more than ninety pounds soaking wet. He was a short man, looked a little bit like Dustin Hoffman, and he never made eye contact with you but rather looked down intently at his feet as if realizing he had grown another toe. He was too slight in build to be dangerous, which gave us comfort knowing if it ever came down to it, Mamma could take him. She met him in church, or rather he was wandering through the hallways looking for a warm place to sleep, when Mamma descended upon him like a vulture on a deer carcass. In a matter of minutes she found out his entire life story, invited him to stay at the house for the holidays, offered to set him up with her neighbor's daughter Viola who was a little on the heavy side but could make a sinfully good pound cake, and even saved him in the same breath. Whether it took or not, who knows. The way I figured it, God had to be watching over that man, to send him a sucker as easy as my mamma.

Mamma claimed Lucas had hit a bottom point in his life. Bottom of the whiskey bottle was more like it, according to Uncle Pete, who would recognize a bum if anybody could. But Mamma held strong and asked us would we have turned Jesus away. I couldn't help wondering if Jesus would have looked like Dustin Hoffman. Anyway, we all figured that it would only take five minutes around Mamma and Lucas Diggs would be running back to the streets. We were wrong.

Not only did Lucas Diggs stick around, he became Mamma's little helper and seemed to love every minute of it. He hung lights, wrapped gifts, painted props, and even joined the choir. Lucas was giving Mamma the kind of Christmas she had always wanted and we hated him for it. Not so much for helping Mamma but for making us look bad in the process. But every time we complained about him, Mamma came back with the same reply: What you do to your neighbor you're doing to Christ.

Lucas even took John Henry's place in helping Mamma with her fruitcake project, not that John Henry minded. You see, every year Mamma spent months baking hundreds of fruitcakes, selling them, and donating the money to the charity of her choosing. As it happened, Mamma had not yet chosen a recipient that year and decided it particularly fitting that the money be given to a foundation for the homeless on Lucas's behalf. At which point she became convinced that God had sent Lucas to her in the form of an angel, elevating him to such a level that after a week she had all of us waiting for him to sprout wings or something.

Mamma and her haggard angel were seen gallivanting all over Cedar Grove selling fruitcakes door to door. They visited the sick, served apple cider to carolers, and collected clothes for the needy. He carried her groceries, peeled potatoes, changed sheets for the company, and polished silver. When relatives started arriving, he carried their bags, hung up their coats, and got them their drinks while they whispered about this disheveled new angel of Mamma's. He blessed the food, carved the turkey, and listened to Aunt Marge's detailed account of her gall bladder surgery that always ended with a viewing of the scar. He helped the little ones put out cookies for Santa and marched around on the roof like reindeer. He even sat with Mamma at the piano and sang Christmas carols with her like a scene straight off a greeting card. I wanted to puke.

Now you may be getting this gut feeling that something's gonna go wrong. That this is one of those Christmas-turned-sour stories where the family wakes up Christmas morning to find Lucas has cleaned them out and then like the Grinch suddenly gets a burst of Christmas spirit and gives everything back. If that's what you're thinking, you're right except for one thing. This Grinch didn't have a change of heart.

I woke up early that Christmas morning and shuffled sleepily through the quiet house to the kitchen, following the smell of coffee. I knew Mamma would be up drinking coffee and reading the Bible. Sometimes I wondered if that woman ever slept at all. I knew she would be sitting by the window, her glasses falling down her nose. It's how I remembered Mamma most, probably because it was the only time I ever saw her sit still. But when I reached the doorway that morning I saw a different sight; Mamma bent over her arms on the kitchen table, her shoulders shaking gently with silent sobs. It was the first time I had ever seen my mother cry.

Sitting in her outstretched hand was the empty coffee can that told me what had happened. It was the can where she kept the fruitcake money. I knew Mamma had gotten up extra early to count that money, just like she did every Christmas. And I knew the money was gone, every penny, and so was Lucas. We had been right about Lucas all along. But for once, it didn't please me to be right. I didn't think it was so much the missing money that hurt Mamma, the money John Henry was supposed to help her raise, but that her angel had betrayed her. As I tiptoed back into my room I couldn't help wondering just how that fit into God's plan.

When I entered the kitchen later, having heard the others up and about, Mamma was back to normal, just a slight puffiness around the eyes as evidence that I hadn't dreamed the whole thing. She didn't mention a word about the money. I knew she didn't want to ruin the day for us. That was Mamma's way, always trying to make the world nice for everybody else. I cringed as I remembered all the hateful things I had said to her in my mind so often over the years. Suddenly I knew what I had to do and I took Uncle Pete and Uncle Frank aside and explained my plan.

We opened gifts in the usual flurry of activity that was tradition in our tiny house on Dove Circle. Surprisingly, Lucas left the gifts. He must have already seen John Henry's monogrammed battery-operated coffee cup warmer. Lucas did take the gift with his name on it, from Mamma, a leather-bound Bible with his initials in gold.

The sounds of ripping paper and squealing children filled the house. We all faked our surprise as we opened the annual knitted sweater from Granny, as predictable as the fact that it would be missing an arm, or a neck hole. Folks oohed and aahed in delight while some eyes raised in confusion at their gift's purpose. In all the chaos, nobody noticed Pete and Uncle Frank slip out the door.

They returned three hours later, their arms filled with shopping bags. They had to drive fifty miles to find a grocery store open on Christmas day. Mamma and Daddy were out helping deliver food to the elder folks so they weren't there to see the rest of us kinfolk gathered together in that tiny kitchen on Dove Circle, rolling up our sleeves and getting down to business. The business of making fruitcakes. You'd have thought it was rocket science the way we went about it. It took Uncle Frank thirty minutes to study the recipe and double check the measurements. To my knowledge, he had never set foot in a kitchen. Aunt Bitsy made us boil all the utensils first on account of she'd just seen a special on this disease called sow monilla. Aunt Vyrnetta was in charge of wrapping the fruitcakes since no one trusted her long fingernails around the mixing bowls. Pete did the chopping, on account of he was an expert with knives, and my little sister Olive was the keeper of the timer, a job she fiercely protected by biting anyone who tried to take it away. Uncle Frank's boss Fritz greased the pans, droning on and on about how they were not fruitcakes for the homeless, but for the dwelling-challenged.

In the course of the day every kitchen utensil had been used, more ingredients had landed on our clothes than actually made it into the mixing bowls, Donald sneezed in the pecans, Pete cut his finger, Aunt Rose saw the blood and passed out cold in the middle of the kitchen floor with such a thud that an entire batch of baking fruitcakes collapsed. Donald ate so much dough he ended up puking and they caught Granny pouring bourbon into the batter. We ran out of sugar and had to use artificial sweetener, which sent Aunt Bitsy into one of her fits on account of she'd just seen this show on aspartame and how it makes you forget, and come to think of it, she had forgotten whipped cream at the market last week, and oh my word, it was starting already, and she got herself so worked up that she had to lie down for a spell. John Henry had a big clump of dough matted to the back of his head exactly where Pete had been aiming and our finished holiday fruitcakes resembled concrete road kill — all fifty-two of them. But to us, they were beautiful.

We loaded up Pete's pickup, bundled up, and started out over the neighborhood to sell our beloved fruitcakes. We hit every place in town with a light on. Folks thought we were joking when we told them they were $30 each, especially when they got a look at 'em. But when we told them about Lucas, the angel gone bad, folks bought the cakes without hesitating. People emptied their pockets and those who had no money gave food or clothes. Folks were helping the homeless, but to most of them it was more than that. They were helping Mamma. It surprised me how many people loved Mamma and were willing to prove it. The woman I considered a leech on my soul.

By the end of the day, we had collected $1,560 and still had six fruitcakes left. We pulled up to the house, honking the horn, laughing and cheering, and yelling for Mamma, singing Christmas carols like we had completely lost our minds. I was singing loudest of all. We found Mamma staring at the kitchen we had left in a complete state of destruction. She turned in surprise and we handed her the money, and she stared at all of our red faces, and looked back at the kitchen and she began to understand. She was shocked and probably wouldn't have believed it if she hadn't seen it herself. For the second time in my life I saw Mamma cry. You could see the pride painted all over her face and I couldn't speak for the rest of 'em but for me it was worth it. For the first time in my life I had done something for Mamma and it felt great. It was the best Christmas I ever had.

We didn't know what became of Lucas Diggs, alias Luther Douglas, alias Lester Davis, except someone saw on that crime show where he was wanted in three states for running the biggest Christmas scam along the East Coast. He had made a career of searching out women just like Mamma. Only after that somewhere along the way he became known as the Bible bandit,

leaving Bibles behind him on every job, which just goes to ⸱
there's some things in life you'll never understand.

That was Mamma's last Christmas. The last one befoᵣ
cancer came calling, as she put it. And before we even had time
to get used to the idea, Mamma was gone, leaving me with only
the memory of her rumbling laugh and the image of her sitting
at the kitchen table, her glasses falling down her nose. Looking
back, I think she knew that was her last Christmas. And that
maybe she saw Lucas Diggs as her last chance to do good on
earth. And despite what anybody thinks, I decided that she did
just that and taught me a valuable lesson in the process.
Sometimes you got to love your neighbor despite their flaws
'cause after all, isn't that what God did for us? And look at the
price He paid.

Some folks would say it was a horrible Christmas and
that Lucas was just another example of what this world is coming
to. But some would say Lucas actually did our family a favor.
Maybe, just maybe, you could say Lucas was that angel Mamma
was always looking for after all. And it was all part of God's
plan. I guess it's all in how you choose to see it.

A Cedar Grove Christmas Carol

Joy to the world,
The Lord has come,
Let earth receive her King.

Every year, Christmas gets bigger and better, flashier and more expensive. But there's one thing about it that never changes – the TV programs. Watching It's a Wonderful Life two hundred and fifty times in your fuzzy feet pajamas, eating warm ginger cookies left over from the ones your Mamma made for Santa. Screaming for joy because Rudolph the Red Nosed Reindeer is on TV and you've only watched it six times this year, and then running around the house with your little brother tied up with the dog collar yelling, "On Dasher, On Dancer." Singing every word to You're a Mean One, Mr. Grinch. Watching Mamma tear up at that same place she always does in Miracle on 34Th Street while your Daddy curses under his breath in the background trying to untangle that string of demon-possessed Christmas lights.

And one of them stories that's been on for as long as I can remember is A Christmas Carol. You remember that story? About Scrooge and the ghost of Christmas past? And little Tim with his crippled leg? Well, you ain't gonna believe this but Cedar Grove's got a story just like that. Okay, maybe some of the details are a tad bit askew, but ain't no denying the resemblance. I call it the Cedar Grove Christmas Carol. Did I ever tell you that story? Well, it all started with a rumor.

It was years before Cedar Grove got swindled by that traveling Bible salesman in the plaid suit, before the flood that wiped out Old Man Byerly's place, and way before Cleetus Harley's pig made front page of the paper. In fact, this was way before Cleetus Harley. Way back to when Alabaster Cripe was the richest man in town.

Anyway, this whole story started with a rumor that Alabaster Cripe was moving his car dealership out of Cedar Grove. This might not be a big deal to you or me but it was a very big deal to the folks in Cedar Grove. Moving the car dealership meant folks out of work, it meant businesses closing up, and it meant they'd never get them that Value Mart they'd been praying so desperately for. Why, there was some folks convinced that once that dealership was gone, the town would up and dry out and disintegrate into a cloud of dust like what happens when you leave an apple peel out on your front stoop to bake in the sun for a couple of months. Folks were fired up to say the least. And what with it being Christmas time and all. Why this rumor was at the very center of every conversation in Cedar Grove from the pink sponge-roller'd terry-cloth clad women talking over the fence, to the gum smacking tobacco spittin' retired men chewing on corn cob pipes in their assigned seats in front of the Five and Dime.

Thing about this rumor though, it was true. Alabaster Cripe did have plans of moving his car dealership out of Cedar Grove and over into Garnett County where he was convinced he could triple his earnings in six months time. He did not give one guinea pig's behind about what that meant to the rest of the folk in town or that it was Christmas time. Made sense if you knew Alabaster. He was downright wicked.

> Alabaster Cripe was a nasty man.
> He was mean beyond belief.
> He never laughed and he never smiled.
> Why, we weren't sure he had teeth
>
> Alabaster Cripe was about this tall
> With a head as bald as a tater,
> A chin like a witch, and an eye that twitched
> And a mood worse than a gator.
>
> Alabaster Cripe he was mean since birth
> And he never missed a day
> But the tide would turn, and he soon would learn
> 'Bout the error of his ways.

Alabaster Cripe hadn't always been the richest man in Cedar Grove. Why, once he was probably considered the poorest. Why, he was once so broke that burglars used to break into his house and leave money. He was so broke he used to wave around a Popsicle stick and call it air conditioning. He was so broke that when they saw him kicking a can down the street and asked him what he was doing, he said, "Moving." Anyway, you get my point. The man was broke.

Alabaster had him a partner named Nester Rimes who he was visiting on the day my story begins. Well, it wasn't actually a visit, Nester had just gotten out of jail and was headed over to the Tasty Freeze for his first thick chocolate milkshake in fifteen years when he ran into Alabaster, who was over in Garnett county meeting with the Chamber of Commerce about moving his dealership over there. When they laid eyes on each other there was static running between them so thick that you could hear it crackle if you were standing close enough. And with good reason if you knew what happened between 'em.

> Nester and Alabaster, peas in a pod,
> Were partners once way back,
> Working their way to be rich some day,
> Both as crooked as a dinosaur's back.
>
> Nester Rimes was a squirrelly sort,
> A man that couldn't be trusted,
> But he got his due, my friends it's true
> Cause the man got himself busted.
>
> And he skipped his bail and he went to jail
> And they threw away the key
> And that's where he sat, imagine that,
> While Alabaster went Scot free.

Now some folks would have bet money that a fight would break out at that moment but then they wouldn't have known about what happened to Nester while he was off doing time. He found the Lord. Or rather the Lord found him if you want to be technical about it. And he changed his ways. Instead of cheating his neighbor he was loving his neighbor. Instead of starting trouble he was now making peace. Instead of hauling off and unleashing a can of kick butt on Alabaster, which he deserved by the way, Nester gave him this warning:

Alabaster man, it's good to see 'ya
But from what I hear it ain't so good to be ya.
Mark my words 'cause I been in your shoes,
I got some advice that you could use.

Your bad deeds are piling up so high
That they're reaching clear up to the sky,
Your life's not been that worthy, I'm told.
Better straighten up man, get back your soul.

You better start now, try and find a way
To righten out the wrongs that you have made,
To make some love out of that hate.
Better change your life before it's too late.

Yeah, like I said, Alabaster started out just as poor as the rest of 'em but somewhere along the way all that changed and he turned into the stingiest, meanest, hair-splittinest, back stabbinest, taking candy from a babyest kind of man that ever stepped foot in Cedar Grove. And cheap to boot. He was so cheap he watered down the coffee in his service department and made the detailers use only use half a bottle of the scented stuff inside the car so's it could stretch out to two. He was so cheap if he took a dollar bill out of his pocket George Washington would blink at the sunlight. Why, he'd steal the coins from a blind man's begging bowl. If he were the type to go to church you can bet he'd put his money into the collection plate and take out change. Yep, that man was cheap. And downright wicked. And flat out empty inside. 'Cause the way folks in Cedar Grove saw it he was missing the very one thing in his life that shouldn't be missing. He was missing the Lord. And wasn't nobody knew that better than Bircham Jones, the number one detailer over at Alabaster's car dealership. But you'll meet Bircham later.

Anyway, Mr. Alabaster Cripe met up with Nester Rimes in the street that day and got that warning about changing his ways. Well, do you think Alabaster up and changed his ways right then and there? Of course not. He was a nasty wicked man with an empty soul. It ain't always that easy to up and change your ways, especially when you like them ways and don't think they need changing.

Alabaster laughed at Nester Rimes. Was still smirking later that night when he settled into his easy chair to sign the papers and watch the news, his favorite television program, especially when there was a tornado or a hurricane wrecking some town. Tonight there was a bombing in some country far off and Alabaster smiled with excitement. Now that was entertainment. I told you he was wicked. He settled into his chair with them papers to sign sitting on his lap. He had all the lights off in case some carolers decided to come by, it being Christmas Eve and all. He didn't want to be bothered. And that's how he commenced to dozing.

It was at some point wee in the morning that his throat felt a little bit scratchy and he went into the kitchen for a soda pop and when he opened up the refrigerator you would not believe what he saw. Sitting right there smack on top of that half-eaten pack of bologna sat Fiona Ray Faynetta Fairy God Mother in Training filing her nails and waiting for this moment. Fiona Ray Faynetta was the real Fairy Godmother's cousin three times removed and twice over and was currently in the middle of one of them Fairy Godmother Correspondence courses and this semester her on-site assignment was the infamous Alabaster Cripe, well known by all Fairy Godmothers in the world who feared the day they would be called on to help that wicked man. But Fiona being from the South was fearless as she blew a bubble and smoothed out another nail.

"Alabaster Cripe," she said. "We gotta talk."

Alabaster wiped his eyes and shook his head thinking he had done lost his mind at the sight of that tiny gum popping woman lounging her feet across his stick of butter. Why nobody was gonna believe this. He tried to speak and he couldn't. Has that ever happened to you in a dream where you try to say something but you can't? Well, that's what happened to Alabaster as his face grew red with anger at this unwanted visitor who was leaving prints in his Margarine. It was freaky.

Now don't you fret and work up a sweat
I'm not saying I'm talking ghost
Or witches or devils or dragon creatures
Or whatever troubles you most

Not premonitions or superstitions
Ain't nothing you can't believe
Just a couple of folks showin' up in a dream
While he slept that Christmas Eve

Fiona sighed impatiently and motioned for Alabaster to come in. Might seem crazy to us, some little fairy godmother in training motioning us to walk into the Frigidaire like it was the most natural thing in all the world. But sometimes dreams don't make sense now do they? So hush up and listen to what happened next.

Alabaster followed her and as he walked in one end of that Frigidaire and they kept on walking right out the back like it had some secret kind of back door. Now that sounds familiar, don't it? Well, anyway, it's my story. And when they walked out the back they walked right into an old dirty shabby looking office with a plasticated plant covered in dust and orange upholstered chairs that clashed hideously with the lime green sofa that had seen better days. And there was a man sleeping on that sofa his back turned to 'em. Alabaster didn't know where he was, I mean he was still trying to get over the fact that he just walked through his refrigerator, but he got this sense that he had been there before.

"It should be familiar," Fiona Ray Faynetta answered his unspoken question. "That's you sleeping on that couch."

"That was the night you got kicked out of your apartment cause you couldn't pay the rent, said Fiona. You didn't have enough coins in your pocket to clang together, hadn't eaten a full meal in weeks, oh but you didn't care. You had hope Mr. Alabaster Cripe. You had dreams. And you had a boss who let you sleep in this office even though it was Christmas Eve and this sleeping man here don't know it yet, but soon that boss man's gonna come and pick you up and take you to his house for a hot turkey meal, and he's gonna give you a promotion and a big old fat Christmas bonus."

"And you swore that day that you would pay him back for all he done, every last cent. And he shook his head and said all he wanted was for you to return the favor one day to someone who needed it. You remember that Alabaster? Didn't happen, did it? Boss man hired Nester Rimes a couple of years later and the two of you got greedy. You kept wanting more. And more. And more. Till you finally turned on each other. It ain't pretty Cripe. What you've done with your life. What happened to that man from long ago?"

Alabaster just stared at the sleeping figure as the memories come flooding back. He had forgotten what it felt like to be poor. He had sworn he'd never feel that way again. And he didn't. He was rich. Stinking filthy rich. Wasn't his fault if nobody was as smart as him. He was rich and that was all that mattered. Wasn't it? And then Alabaster found himself sitting right back in his recliner and Fiona Ray Faynetta was just a memory.

He was kind of shaking a little bit on account of on the dream scale that hit the top of the freaky chart. And he thought that was the end of it. But it wasn't 'cause in the blink of an eye standing not two feet away warming his hands on the fire, none other than Jolly Old Saint Nicholas, Santa Claus, St. Nick, Kris Cringle, the jolly big guy in red, whatever you want to call him, but you all know who I'm talking about. Way Alabaster figured it, had to be Santa what with the red suit and the long white beard and the big belly that shook when he laughed like a bowl full of jelly. If that wasn't Santa Claus then that robber was seriously fashion challenged. "Ho – ho – ho Alabaster Cripe," said the jolly man in red. Yep, Santa Claus. What did I tell ya! Only this Santa Claus was anything but jolly. And once again old Alabaster is speechless. Smart thinking on behalf of whoever planned that dream because as wicked as Alabaster was you wouldn't want him to let loose on Santa Claus. Ain't nobody supposed to pick on Santa, dream or not.

"Alabaster, Alabaster," Santa shook his head sadly from side to side. "This is supposed to be a happy night for me, delivering toys and presents to all the children. But folks aren't smiling in this town Alabaster. Folks are worried about losing their jobs and not being able to make ends meet. And there's one house where things are particularly overcast. One house where Christmas isn't anything special. And Mr. Cripe, you have just about everything to do with that." And in the blink of an eye Alabaster and Santa were standing in the home of Bircham Jones next to the hairy looking Christmas tree with paper decorations as Bircham and Emmadine Jones sat at the table praying for a Christmas miracle. Alabaster could have sworn he'd met that man before.

Bircham Jones was the detailer over at Alabaster's dealership. He was a tall thin man with an Adam's apple that bobbed up and down like the lure on a fishing line. The lines in his face told a story of hard work and hard times but his eyes held a sparkle that showed life hadn't gotten him down. They were eyes that said you can take away all I have, but you can't take away this sparkle in my eye. Anyway, Bircham Jones was a good man. Some folks called him a simple man and if you believe like I do, you consider that a compliment.

> Bircham Jones had a friendly soul
> And his friends they called him Birch
> Cause he looked like a tree much taller 'n me
> And the nickname, well, just worked
>
> Bircham Jones was a good-hearted soul
> Sweet smile like pumpkin spice
> If you needed a hand, he was your man
> And you didn't have to ask him twice
>
> His life was hard you could tell by his face
> How the lines were deep and long
> Money was tight and worries were big
> But his faith was always strong
>
> There was just one thing that'd get him down
> Just find his wife and ask her
> That one life toil that would plague his soul
> Was his boss man, Alabaster

Anyway, Bircham was praying with his wife Emmadine Jones. She had her own nail painting booth over at Myrlene, Vyrlene and Shirlene's House Of Beauty and was doing pretty good at it truth be told till that little fungus episode. Wasn't her fault really, I mean it was before folks knew as much as they do now about hygiene and all, and it was only one person who had it at first, but I guess one is all it takes. And I tell you what, can't nothing spread through a town faster than a nail fungus. Only thing faster than the spreading nail fungus was news of the spreading fungus that burned up the phone lines clear over to Garnett County. Fastest business gone belly up in history and Emmadine Jones was out of a job. Which just meant more troubles for that poor family. And oh how Emmadine would worry.

> Emmadine Jones was Bircham's wife
> Prettiest thing you've ever seen
> His high school sweet, swept him off his feet
> Miss Cedar Grove Sweet Potato Queen
>
> Oh she loved her Birch, he was her man
> But how that woman would complain
> She was one of them types of people who
> Miss the rainbow for the rain
>
> What're we gonna do Birch? What're we gonna do?
> Emmadine Jones would cry
> And she'd wring her freshly polished nails
> And wonder how they'd all get by

Twig and Sarah (the Jones younguns) were over in the corner wrapping presents with leftover newspaper they found in someone's trash. Alabaster noticed the wrapping on Twig's foot and the cane propped up against the fireplace. I think Twig was about seven that year, and his real name was Bircham Jones Junior. Since his pa was called Birch it was only fitting that folks called his son Birch Junior only folks kept getting them mixed up, and then it turned into little Birch, and then someone with a pretty quick wit called him Twig, and well it just stuck like nicknames have a way of doing. Twig was something of a troublemaker though his heart was always in the right place. You just couldn't help but love him. Only at the time my story takes place, folks looked at Twig different — with the kind of look you'd give a dog who's only got three legs. Let me explain.

Twig had a habit of keeping his shoes untied which is not such an unusual thing for a kid but there's a reason adult folk are always bugging younguns to keep their shoes tied. Maybe not exactly for the reason that Twig learned but we won't get that technical about it. Anyway, Twig had been begging his pa for months to let him drive that new John Deere tractor of Grandpa's which was sitting in the backyard till they got it sold. Grandpa had decided couple months back that life just wasn't complete without a John Deere. Might have made sense if he was a farmer or even owned some land. But Grandpa lived in one of them high rise retirement communities somewheres up North and obviously had too much time on his hands 'cause he spent most nights watching that shopping channel and a lonely man with a credit card ain't a good combination. And, well, you can figure out the rest.

Anyway, Twig had been begging his father to let him drive that tractor that was just sitting in the backyard collecting dust. And his father always said no. So Twig did what lots of boys would do I reckon. He drove it when his pa wasn't home. And maybe that thirty second spin around the backyard might not have been such a big deal but forgetting to tie his shoelaces was. And let's just say that terrible little story ends with Twig losing his foot. Folks said he was lucky to be alive. Twig thought he'd rather be dead than to walk around with only one foot. The only hope was that there was talk about them fancy plastic limbs being made over in Garnett County. But even Twig being a kid knew not to get his hopes up. They just didn't have the money. Plain and simple. Not on what Alabaster paid his Pa and being as how Emmadine's nail business was now a bust. So Twig got quieter and quieter, and sadder and sadder.

> Twig I'm told was a restless soul
> Couldn't sit to save his life
> He was here then there, he was everywhere
> Like a firefly in mid-flight

But one day he was made to pay
Learned a lesson sad but true
'Bout the price you pay when you disobey
What your parents tell you to

Yes Twig lost himself a foot that year
Don't feel sorry for him not one bit
We all got troubles in our life at times
And we gotta make the best of it

Twig's sister Sarah was a fiery spirited redhead who was ten going on thirty. She was the only one who didn't baby Twig. She said she didn't care if he had a one foot or three, he was still acting like a ninny and that's why kids whispered behind his back. Sarah was known for telling it like it was.

"Good grief," thought Alabaster, "this should be on a Hallmark card. It's enough to make me wanna puke. Oh, my aching heart," he thought, trying to remember where he'd seen that man before.

"He works for you," said Santa, shaking his head. "Bircham Jones – do you even know his name, Alabaster? And that's his wife Emmadine, and Twig, and Sarah. Did you know Twig lost his foot this year? Did you know they can't even make the medical payments much less pay the rest of their bills? Did you know only thing Twig asked for this year was a new foot? They don't have a turkey for Christmas, they'll be lucky to have anything. And now they've heard that you plan to move the dealership. That will mean Bircham will be out of a job. And do you know what they're doing right now? They're praying, Alabaster. Ever heard of that?"

Alabaster felt a twinge of something he figured was probably just heartburn and was desperately wishing he was back in his easy chair watching the news. And that's when he heard it. Just a simple sentence that rang through the night and wrapped around his wicked old heart. "And please," said Bircham Jones in his deep voice, "please God if you would kindly bless Mr. Alabaster Cripe. He surely does need it."

Alabaster was stunned. To his knowledge nobody had ever prayed for him before. And of all people, this detailer from his own dealership who had every reason to despise him. Shoot, Alabaster didn't even know who the man was and golly darn if that man wasn't sitting there praying for him. Alabaster felt another twinge of that heartburn. I like to think it was pieces of his icy heart starting to chip away but then I tend to be a bit dramatic about things. And in a blink of an eye Alabaster was sitting back in his recliner and Santa had disappeared. leaving behind a pair of new slippers just Alabaster's very size, the only evidence that he was even there at all.

Alabaster's head was spinning and his pulse was racing. I guess that can happen when you get one of them reality checks. And that's when the donkey showed up. Can't remember his name, but he was gray and kind of funny looking.

"You Mister Cripe?" the donkey asked, pressing his nose in Alabaster's face and breathing hot donkey breath on him. Alabaster nodded thinking that this was like a nightmare on Fairy Tale street. He still couldn't speak. which was a good thing 'cause that donkey could talk enough for three people. "Your Cripeness, I am here to show you what the future holds for a nasty man such as yourself. Fiona done showed you what you used to be, and Santy Nick done showed you what you is, and now I' m here to show you what you gonna be if you keep going in the direction you're going. I swear I ain't never seen the actions of one man cause so much trouble down the line except for Adam, and Alabaster you is much meaner than Adam now that's a man knows all about the domino effect of just one solitary misdeed. Oh, but that Eve now, she was a looker. No wonder she talked him into eating that apple, she was a hottie, why she could have talked an Eskimo into buying a cooling system. Anyway, take a look around you Cripe Master and see if you can guess where you are."

Alabaster looked around at the town, or what used to be a town. He was standing directly in the middle of the deserted street. It was like one of them westerns where the cowboy walks directly through the center of town and the only sign of life is tumbleweed floating across the street. Well, that's what it felt like to Alabaster.

"Feels like a ghost town, don't it?" said the donkey. "Why you can almost hear the Gunsmoke music, can't you? I swear I keep expecting Clint Eastwood to turn that corner up there. Dried up is what this town is, old Cripe the Gripe. Dried up version of Cedar Grove. That used to be Ray Jean's Diner – even the cockroaches have moved out. And over there's where you used to play as a kid while your mamma picked up her sewing supplies. See that lot over yonder behind the Baptist Church that finally closed its doors when the only standing there was the pastor. Kind of hard to have an altar call, if you know what I mean."

"The lot with all the tombstones. That's where they put you, Alabaster. Can't believe they even bothered to give you a funeral. Didn't matter, nobody came. Not one single person, Mr. Alabaster. Barely had enough money to afford a tombstone. That's why it says Tot Jones on it. They got a deal 'cause it was supposed to be for Tom Jones but that's when Skeeter had some issues with the bottle and, well, he just wasn't all put together right when it come time to make that tombstone and it came out Tot Jones. And they couldn't use it cause it says Tot. Figured you wouldn't care or even know for that matter. You didn't have any family or friends to speak of and no money. You lost all that in something called the stock market. Anyway, that fencepost over yonder is where you fell off and split your chin open and had a couple of stitches put in and you told everybody you got it from apprehending a criminal. That was when you were interesting and fun, Your Cripeness. Now you're just mean and nasty. And the only one to blame for the death of Cedar Grove. How does that make you feel, your nastiness? Couldn't feel good."

> Look around you Alabaster Cripe
> What more do I got to say
> To help you see realistically
> The kind of man you are today
>
> Look around you Alabaster Cripe
> At the way this town will be
> All because of you and the things you do
> Change things permanently

It ain't a pretty picture Mister Cripe
Not a friend to call your own
You're stingy and mean and selfish in between
Won't even give a dog a bone

Women won't date 'ya, employees all hate ya
Your neighbors want to see you dead
Even the postman hates your mail
Least that's what the milkman said

I gotta tell you this old Mister Cripe
You better listen up and listen good
You only get one turn at this sweet life
So you better try and make it good

'Cause the day will come, to all not some
When they're gonna call your ticket in
And someone will look in a golden book
To see what kind of man you've been

And I hate to say it but I can't delay it
It's a shame I got to be the one
To tell you it's true but the page on you
Well, your good deeds are all but none

But consider you lucky Mr. Cripe
It appears you get you one more chance
To use this day to evaluate your way
To change your little song and dance

And now Mr. Cripe I'm checking out
Got other places that I must be
Can't say it was a treat for us to meet
Just hope you listened to us three.

And in the blink of an eye Alabaster was sitting back in his easy chair — alone. I *t was just a dream. Didn't mean anything. Bunch of crazy nonsense. Probably something you ate for dinner.* But sometimes it's hard to lie to yourself. Especially if it's just you and yourself that's doing the talking. And Alabaster sat in that cold dark room on Christmas Eve with them papers sitting in his lap waiting to be signed and he could hear the carolers next door and their voices faintly carrying a tune through the air that he hadn't heard in a long time. Joy to the world. And he felt like they were singing that song just for him. And if you want to believe it, well, maybe they were. *Joy to the world, the Lord has come, Let Earth receive her King.* And them words that he'd heard a half a million times dove right straight through the middle of his cold empty heart and filled it up.

And suddenly Alabaster didn't care that he was the richest man in Cedar Grove. He cared that he was the meanest. And suddenly he didn't care that he could make three times more money over in Garnett County. He cared that Twig and Sarah had to wrap their Christmas gifts in newspaper. And he didn't care about who might be cheatin' him. He cared about who he might be cheatin' and I think you know who I'm talking about. And Alabaster's wicked nasty heart sang out in joy and the room was filled with brightness that didn't come from the fire. *Joy to the world. The Lord has come. Let Earth receive her king. Let every heart prepare him room. And heaven and nature sing.* And for the first time in Alabaster's life he fell to his knees and cried like a baby. Much like I'm gonna do if this story lasts much longer.

> Christmas morning in Cedar Grove
> Was crisp and clear and bright
> They celebrated a savior's birth
> Born in a manger's light
>
> But the biggest surprise to folks that year
> Running through streets at dawns first light
> Yelling a Merry Christmas to all
> None other than Alabaster Cripe
>
> Knocking on doors with gifts galore
> Money and toys for every tot
> He spent the day much that same way
> Wasn't one place that man forgot

Twig got himself a foot that year
Bircham Jones got a new promotion
Emmadine Jones got a beauty salon
But the biggest cause for commotion

Was when Alabaster Cripe apologized
To every person in town he'd wronged
And said the dealership was here to stay
And you could bet his promise was strong

Why in Cedar Grove that Christmas day
Angels sang in heavn'ly harmony
Story's sweetest part is a changing heart
Why there ain't no better testimony

Fiona Ray Faynetta earned her Fairy status
Santa Claus is happy once again
The donkey's still talking Twig is back walking
And this is where the story ends.

Joy to the world, the Lord has come.
Let earth receive her king.
Let every heart, prepare him room,
and heaven and nature sing,
and heaven and nature sing.

Three Weeks Left To Live

Did I ever tell you the story about John Henry Junior and the time he found out he only had three weeks left to live? Before I do, I best make sure you're familiar with a term known to most as eavesdropping. Eavesdropping is when you listen in on a conversation that don't belong to you, and according to my mamma, a very rude thing to do.

John Henry had heard talk about life being short and all; he just never knew how short it could be, 'til that dreadful Saturday morning when he found out he only had three weeks left to live. Which brings me to the beginning of my story, when John Henry happened to stumble on a conversation between his mamma and Ray Jean Jones.

One thing you learn quick as a kid, when adult folk are whispering it's usually on account of they don't want you to hear what they're saying. And if they don't want you to hear what they're saying, why there's a good chance that it's something awful exciting, maybe even you they're talking about. So when John Henry walked past that closed kitchen and heard them hushed voices why he couldn't resist planting his ear upside the door. And that's how he commenced to eavesdropping.

"Only three weeks left to live. Horrible thing, I tell you." Ray Jean's raspy voice was loud even for a whisper. She had the biggest mouth this side of the river – a mouth that couldn't hold secrets any better than a brand spanking new pup can hold his bark, if you know what I mean.

"My word, that's just awful," said Suga, John Henry's mamma. John Henry's mind raced, wondering who it was only had three weeks left to live. Maybe it's old man Peterson. He was so old they said he once played chess with Noah. Or maybe his cousin Myra. Folks were always swearing that one day her mouth would be the death of her. He strained to hear more.

"Crying shame – and so young too. Pass me one more of those muffins dear. Anyway, thought you should be the first to know," said Ray Jean. Wonder how many people she's already said that to, thought John Henry. Somebody young. Now if that don't change everything! Who could it be? The new Henderson baby? He is always throwing up all over people. Or maybe Percy Wintergreen who lives with his granny over on Fifth Street. Mamma's always saying that woman's gonna kill that youngun feeding him all that fat back. John Henry was so wrapped up in that conversation that a line of juggling circus clowns could have passed by and he wouldn't have noticed.

"Doc found it in his check-up last week," Ray Jean continued. "Wrote right there in the medical report only nobody knows about it yet." John Henry knew with Ray Jean Jones involved, everybody in Cedar Grove would know about it by lunch. Suddenly his whole body went numb with horror. Wait! I had a checkup last week!

"Say's he'll be feeling real tired. And loss of appetite," said Ray Jean. John Henry grabbed the wall as the room spun around him. He didn't finish his dinner last night, and come to think of it, he had been feeling a bit tired lately.

"Says they knew by the spots," said Ray Jean dramatically. John Henry stifled a scream as he saw a tiny red dot on his arm he'd never seen before. It's me! Me! I only got three weeks left to live! Now, finding out you only got three weeks can be a tough thing for anybody to swallow, but for a kid, well, it can be down right devastating. He ran out of the house and down the street as fast as he could, straight to Luther's. Cause after all, when something like this happens to you, first place you go is to your best friend. He charged up the stairs to Luther's room, tears running down his face, choking on his words as he told Luther the horrible news.

"I'm dying. I'm dying," John Henry wailed, moaning like a she-cow giving birth. Luther listened intently as John Henry spilled out his story in between sobs – a story that would make no sense to anybody but a best friend.

"Are you sure?" Luther asked. He'd never known anybody with only three weeks left to live before. John Henry nodded, imagining all his relatives screaming and crying and throwing themselves over his coffin like they did at Great Aunt Lilly's funeral.

"Wow," said Luther. After all, what do you say to somebody who's only gonna be around for three more weeks?

"Do you think they'll throw you a party or something?" You could hear John Henry wailing clear over in Garnett County. Luther wasn't exactly the smartest kid that ever lived.

"I'm gonna die. I'm gonna die," John Henry cried and ran to the mirror to see if'n he was looking any different.

"Do you have to go to school anymore?" asked Luther. "Not much point in going to school for just three more weeks." John Henry pondered this new revelation. "And I guess you won't have to do chores or nothing. Folks ain't gonna make you work if you only got three weeks left to live." John Henry nodded, thinking it was a good thing he hadn't cleaned out old man Peterson's stables yet like he promised. "And I bet they'll let you have all the candy and sweets you want, cause they'll be feeling real sorry for you." John Henry almost smiled and Luther was proud to find such a bright side to John Henry's tragedy. "Course, you'll miss Christmas," he said without thinking and John Henry burst into another fit of tears. So much for the bright side.

"Hey, John Henry," exclaimed Luther. "You gotta do one of them 'Willin' Tessments.' My Uncle Frank, when he died, he left a Willin' Tessment." Luther nodded emphatically, suddenly a full authority on the subject.

"A what?" asked John Henry.

"A Willin' Tessment," said Luther, pleased that he knew something John Henry didn't. "It's where you write down all your belongings and who you want to give 'em to after you're gone." John Henry frowned. He didn't like the idea of giving away his stuff.

"That's how I got the gold watch on a chain Nana won't let me touch," said Luther. "She says it's like having something to remember Uncle Frank by, only I don't really remember him 'cause I only met him once." John Henry wasn't listening. He was running out the door shouting for Luther to follow him. This, my friends, is where the real trouble started.

"Go find me a piece of paper, Luther," said John Henry sitting in the middle of his bedroom floor surrounded by all the stuff they could pull out in an hour's time. "And something to write with." Luther came back carrying a notebook and a purple crayon. "I couldn't find a pen," he mumbled. He was kind of mad at John Henry for ordering him around but he didn't say anything – what with him dying and all.

"I can't write a Willin' Tessment with a purple crayon!" John Henry exclaimed, like Luther was an idiot. But it was all they had, so they decided a Willin' Tessment written in purple crayon would just have to do. John Henry started to write.

> *My softball trophy and baseball mitt, I leave to*
> *my best friend, Luther P. Hawkins.*
> Luther beamed.
> *My school picture, I leave to Ma 'cause she says*
> *it's the only time I've ever looked like an angel.*
> *My framed picture of Babe Ruth, I leave to Pa*
> *cause it was his to begin with.*
> *I leave all my toys to my brothers, William Henry*
> *and Benjamin Henry. Don't fight over 'em.*
> *To my sister Ruth Ann, I leave all my collard*
> *greens and school books.* (They agreed that was
> the perfect gift for an obnoxious bratty sister.)
> *To my baby sister Olive, I leave my bed on account*
> *of she's already climbing out of her crib.*
> *I leave my tube socks to my granny since she's*
> *the one who gives 'em to me every year. And the*
> *blue ribbon I stole from Sally Weathersby when*
> *she beat me in the spelling bee – I leave to*
> *anybody but Sally Weathersby.*
> *Yours truly,*
> *Jonathan Abraham Henry, Junior*

"There, that should do it," said John Henry admiring his work.

"What about your bike?" asked Luther who felt bad for him and all, but couldn't help wondering what was to become of that new bike John Henry got for Christmas. John Henry froze. He hadn't thought about giving away his new bike, and didn't want to think about it neither – dead or not. But he couldn't take it with him could he? Nah, he didn't remember reading anything about bike riding in heaven. He sighed deeply and added,

> *P.S. And my new bike, I leave to my best friend,*
> *Luther P. Hawkins, as long as he don't go leaving*
> *it out in the rain or nothing.*

"Wow, thanks John Henry," said Luther, imagining himself coasting through the streets of Cedar Grove, the shiny tassles blowing in the wind. "Can I ride it today?" John Henry had never let him ride it before, and judging by the look on his face, was not about to start.

"I ain't even dead yet and you're already wanting my bike," John Henry yelled. "Some best friend you are. You better be nice to me or I'll take it back and give it to Jimmy Weathersby!" Luther gasped at the horrible thought of giving that five-year-old runny-nosed-tattle-taled-brat the coolest bike in Cedar Grove. "And I don't see as it would hurt if you started doing my chores. Seeing as how I ain't got much time left." John Henry put on his best feel-sorry-for-me face. Luther nodded painfully. He really wanted that bike. And that's when John Henry's eyes lit up. The same look he got whenever he had a plan. It was a look Luther knew well cause it usually ended up with a whupping somewhere along the line. But he couldn't resist listening to John Henry's idea of making people earn his stuff. As usual, John Henry didn't give a second's thought to whether it was right or wrong. Not even an hour later, word had spread among Cedar Grove kidfolk and they were lined up down the street to find out what John Henry would be leaving 'em and what they'd have to do to get it. As you might guess, John Henry's ma and pa were not at home at the time.

"Sam, you can have my army knife, but you gotta take me to the circus next week instead of your cousin," said John Henry perched in a rocking chair on his front porch, surrounded by all his possessions like a king on his throne. Sam nodded eagerly.

"Norma, you can have my telescope but you gotta clean out the stables for old man Peterson, and he likes you to rub down his horse too." Norma cradled her new telescope gingerly. John Henry didn't tell her it was broken.

"Pete, you can have my new jeans, cause you're the only one my size, but you gotta let me have your new puppy for a week." Pete did not want to part with his new puppy but he didn't want to be left out of the Willin' Tessment either, so he agreed.

And the rest of the day went like that. John Henry trading his possessions for things he wanted from the other kids. He gave away everything he could find, even his goldfish, and when he ran out of his own stuff, he grabbed stuff out of the house that wasn't even his and started giving away that. And what a sight it was, kids walking down the street carrying all sorts of items from the Henry household, which is just about the time John Henry's mamma come driving down the street with this puzzled look on her face 'cause she could have sworn she just saw younguns pass by carrying her new blender, and her ironing board, and her tea kettle, and even her pink polka-dotted house dress. And though she didn't know the particulars, she was quite certain her troublemaking son was behind it.

You could hear the screaming all over the neighborhood as his mamma ran up those stairs, jerked John Henry out of that rocker, dragged him into the house by his ear, and slammed the front door so hard Luther thought it would fall off the hinges. John Henry didn't even see it coming and couldn't figure out why she was carrying on so. What with him dying and all, why you'd think she would have been a little bit nicer.

But no sir, she wasn't feeling sorry for him. Not even close. Just one look into those angry eyes of hers and John Henry knew he was in trouble something fierce, and suddenly his bright idea didn't sound so bright anymore, and he started wailing as he realized that now not only was he dying, but he was probably gonna get a whupping too, and he wasn't sure just which was worse.

It took him about an hour to get the whole story out in between sobs about his Willin' Tessment and the spots and being young and three weeks to live and missing Christmas. And his mamma was terribly confused until Ray Jean's name came up and she started piecing the story together. Only she wasn't looking any nicer about it. "You mean you were eavesdropping on me and Ray Jean this morning?" she asked in a way that did not sound like she felt sorry for him, but more like she wanted to rip his head off.

"Yeah," said John Henry in a tiny voice. His mamma nodded slowly and stood there for a minute without saying a word while John Henry watched that vein throb on her neck. She took a deep breath and told him he was right, somebody did only have three weeks to live – Hubert – old man Byerly's prize-winning bull. And then she went on to say that he should know better than to believe everything he heard, 'specially when it wasn't aimed for his ears in the first place. And then she went on to say that even if he was dying, it gave him no right to be making people earn his stuff, much less giving away things that didn't even belong to him, and now his mamma had worked up such a temper, she said those kids could keep every last one of his belongings, including that new bike, and maybe that would teach him not to go nosing in where he didn't belong.

And so that's how Luther came to be the proud new owner of the shiniest coolest bike in Cedar Grove. For about two hours. Until his Nana caught wind of the whole thing and said he was as much to blame as anybody so she gave the bike to none other than little Jimmy Weathersby, that five-year-old runny-nosed tattle-tale, which was about the worst part of it all.

And that's where the story ends. John Henry stayed out of trouble after that – for a couple of days anyway, and then he was off into some other mischief. But folks still tell that story about the day John Henry Jr. found out he only had three weeks left to live, only the closest he came to dying was the whupping he got that night.

And that's all for now.

About Cedar Grove...

Cedar Grove is a tiny town about a mile and a hair past nowhere. They've got two stoplights total, an old brick schoolhouse that also serves as the town hall and bingo headquarters on Thursdays. They're very proud of their one-half of a fast food restaurant. The other half is technically in Butner. Not the same Butner to which you may be familiar with. Time rolls at a slow pace in Cedar Grove, where the most exciting thing that ever happened was the time Cleetus Harley's pig made front page of the paper for having borned her a piglet with three tails. These stories aren't fancy. They're just about the people.

Kelly's stories are filled with humor and wit as they deliver messages of faith and inspiration as seen through the eyes of Cedar Grove, that tiny Southern town about a mile and a hair past nowhere. Her beloved quirky characters will make you laugh and cry at the same time. These are people you know, people you live with, people you can relate to. Their delicious simplicity speaks of a day gone by and reminds us of the important things in life.

About Kelly Swanson . . .

To fully appreciate Kelly's gift is to watch her perform. Her delivery is one of enthusiasm and contagious energy that holds her audiences captive and leaves them wanting more. With only the slightest change in expression, she is transformed into yet another beloved character. You don't see Kelly, you see the people in Cedar Grove. You don't feel entertained, you feel changed.

Kelly lives in High Point, North Carolina, with her husband Bill. Her CD (*Aunt Vyrnetta and other Stories from Cedar Grove*) is now available by phone or on her website.

For Booking Information:
Kelly Swanson
336-889-9479
www.kellyswanson.net
kelly@kellyswanson.net
1400 Chatham Drive
High Point, NC 27265

Kelly Swanson is one of the best comedians I've ever seen. She crosses the generation gap like no comedian I've ever seen and her stories are clean. The characters in Kelly's stories are the people who live right down the street. They're the children, parents, grandparents, aunts, uncles, and cousins that embarrass their own children and provide the fodder of great entertainment. Her stories are down home, and even though outrageous and imagined, you can still believe they just might be real. Each story is like a great book compressed to about fifteen minutes, loaded with laughter, and recorded in Kelly's own wonderful voice. She repeatedly brings her audiences closer and closer to the finish only to pull them away for a few more minutes of genuine Southern humor like few entertainers are able to do these days. Kelly's CD and book, AUNT VYRNETTA ...and other stories from Cedar Grove, is a collection that no lover of clean Southern humor should ever do without.

Billy Jones
Editor / Publisher
Idle Hands Magazine
www.idlehandsmag.com

Told in authentic vernacular, her stories sing with wit and wisdom and wonderful insight into the human condition. Long experience as a writer has honed Kelly's skill as a wordsmith, and when she assumes the role of oral storyteller, that skill is abundantly evident. With a wink and a shout, a whisper and a shake, Kelly's storytelling takes on a life of its own. A terrific teller! Fresh, creative, incredibly woven stories, a little reminiscent of the humorous style of Ferroll Sams, or a livelier Garrison Keillor. Fabulous characterizations. Don't miss the opportunity to see and hear her tell.

Elizabeth Guy
Member, NC Storytelling Guild

Her "Down Home" style is warm and reminiscent of a female Mark Twain.

Mr. Terry A. Rollins
2002-03 President
NC Storytelling Guild

Printed in the United States
15555LVS00005B/367-489